To Ninga —

Enjoy Michael's love story!

2017

So

sweet

REBEKAH WEATHERSPOON

Haven

Books by Rebekah

VAMPIRE SORORITY SISTERS
Better Off Red
Blacker Than Blue
Soul to Keep

STAND ALONES
The Fling
At Her Feet
Treasure

THE FIT TRILOGY
Fit
Tamed
Sated

SUGAR BABY NOVELLAS
So Sweet
So Right
So For Real

Praise for Rebekah's work

"There are actually more really great romance authors out there, but it's only every now and then that you come across writing that makes you say, "This author is going places." Rebekah Weatherspoon is one of those authors." - Pandora Esperanza, *The Last Word Book Reviews*

AT HER FEET

"Indeed, the more I read *At Her Feet* I came to realize that it is the best and most original book that I have read in any genre for a very long time." – Jim Lyon, *The Seattle PI*

FIT

"I felt satisfied by a complete story at the end, and would highly recommend this to anyone looking for a fun, relatable contemporary romance." - Elisa Verna, *Romantic Times Book Reviews (TOP PICK REVIEW)*

TAMED

"The second in Weatherspoon's Fit series, "Tamed" is another must-read for fans of BDSM romance. - Elisa Verna, *Romantic Times Book Reviews (TOP PICK REVIEW)*

TREASURE

"This story is rich yet beguiling, magnificent yet down to earth, and intriguing yet heartwarmingly human." – J.J., *Rainbow Book Reviews*

Dedication

To TL, for suggesting that
I write something just for you.
You've created a monster. I hope you're happy.

And to KB and AR. Thank you for sticking by me.

Chapter One

I was so numb, sitting behind the wheel of my car. The AC was cranked, blowing an excessive amount of cold air across my face, but I couldn't bring myself to turn it down. Over thirty applications, and ten interviews, and I was no closer to finding a new job. My savings were running low and I was one rent check away from kissing the rest of my severance pay goodbye. Unemployment was helping, but if I didn't find something soon…

I knew what would happen. I'd worked so damn hard. Gotten my degree, landed a job as a corporate HR clerk with one of the larger cellphone carriers. The job was as boring as hell and a complete waste of my education, but the pay was good enough to support my lifestyle and I'd learned a lot about the corporate world. I was paying off my student loans, living in a spacious apartment that I loved and, three weeks before they canned me, I'd picked up my first new car.

Over the past few months I'd fantasized about going to the dealership and just giving it back, like that sort of thing happened without adding major blotches on your credit. I'd have these moments, like this moment in traffic where I wondered what would happen if things got that far, if I was forced into true survival mode. I would hear my mom's voice in my head. "You gotta do what you gotta do, baby girl."

A loud blaring horn snapped me out of my trance. The light was green.

Maybe things wouldn't be so bad if my roommate wasn't out of a job too. Adler had worked as a personal assistant to Greg Wilson, a producer at Hourmark Studios. After four monumental flops at the box office he'd been forced out and, during his impassioned exit, taken Adler with him. It didn't take long for his emotional spiral to land him in rehab, leaving his wife and kid with no source of income and Adler without a job. She was helping pay for food and other bills, but her savings were running dangerously low too.

Both of us had emotionally supportive parents, but we'd both come from small towns where everything was cheaper than life in L.A. When I had a job, I made more money than my mom and my half of the rent was more than my parents' mortgage. They could offer long distance hugs, but not a dime to get Adler and me through this. At least not enough dimes to help us keep up with our current living situation. We were so fucked.

Adler was waiting for me when I walked in the door. I'm sure the answers to all of her questions were written all over my face. "Oh fuck. What happened?"

I threw my purse down on the couch and looked up at the ceiling. I was not going to cry. "They didn't even interview me."

"What? Why?"

"I was waiting in the lobby and the interviewer

comes out with this guy and they're laughing and having a grand old time. The guy leaves and the receptionist introduces me to Christian, the guy I'm interviewing with, and he just goes, 'Oh, I'm sorry Miss David—"

"He called you Miss David?"

"Yeah! The girl said Davis and he still got it wrong. So I guess he hired the guy before me on the spot. He kinda apologized and I just turned around and came home."

"Okay. Well that decides it, right?"

"Decides what?"

"Kayla, I'm signing up with Arrangements again."

"Ads, no." I flapped my arms out of sheer frustration.

"I've done it once and I can do it again."

In college Adler had signed up with Arrangements, a dating site that matched college girls with wealthy men who wanted to support them, basically in exchange for sex. After a few duds Adler had been matched up with an oil tycoon who'd paid off her school loans and then promptly died on top of her four months after graduation. She'd found humor in the situation. The guy was old, after all, but her laughter died when it dawned on her that Jed hadn't left her any cash.

"I'm a little rusty, but I think I still got what it takes."

"You say it like you're a breath away from menopause. You're twenty-three."

"I don't know, deary." She licked her lips like

she didn't have any teeth. "This pussy isn't as tight as it used to be."

It felt good to laugh, but I still didn't like the idea. "I don't know."

"I'll just throw my hat back into the ring. It's not as bad as it sounds. I get to pick the guy I date. And if I can't find anyone, I'll try something else. Or wait a bit and try again."

"We can strip," I joked. I wasn't very coordinated in ultra-high heels.

"That's not a bad idea. You'd be good at it. I've seen that ass jiggle. You got plenty to shake. Yeah, girl." I rolled my eyes after she rolled her hips and shimmied her shoulders.

"I know, it's a gift. I still think Arrangements is a bad idea."

"Why? We need money. Some old man will give us money. We will use that money for goods and services. And rent."

"Can't I just be worried?"

"You just think every man is a murderer."

"Every man is a murderer. You're gonna get *murderered*." I pretended to sob as I flopped down on the couch beside her.

"You should do it with me."

"What? No."

"Why not?"

"Um let's see." I gestured to her slim figure. "Cute, petite white girl." Then I gestured to myself and my not-so-perfectly tailored skirt suit. "Chunky-plus black girl. The type of rich guys I would attract are still bitter about slavery ending."

Adler snorted. "You are freaking beautiful. And you are not chunky."

Adler wasn't completely wrong. I was cute as hell. I'd always had super clear skin and I'd inherited my dad's to-die-for dimples. Thanks to some referrals at work I'd found a great woman to do my sew-ins. The eighteen inches of Brazilian Remy I was currently sporting were styled to perfection. I knew how to dress myself, but I was definitely on the plus-size side of things. I attracted a certain kind of man, the older creepier uncle types that hung around gas stations during the day and definitely didn't have enough money to cover our rent.

"I doubt there are any daddies made of sugar who'd want to sugar me," I said.

"Oh yeah they would. Sugar right all over those double D's."

"You are the worst."

"Just think about it. I'm signing up today. At the very least I get no bites. Best case, I find a great guy who wants to shower me with rent money and diamonds."

"Will you share your diamonds with me?" I asked with a pout.

Adler just barely touched my cheek. "You know I will."

"Great. Diamonds or no, I don't think you should do it." I kicked off my kitten heels and headed for the kitchen. "Is there any pizza left?" I asked as I went.

"No..." That stopped me in my tracks. Adler looked extra guilty when I turned around. "I ate it.

But I think there's still some minute noodles."

"Just what I need for the old blood pressure."
Still, I went to the kitchen and put some water on.
Food, shower, and then back to the job boards.

I decided to give myself a break, just for the night. I
had to take a deep breath, clear my mind of the job
interview that never was, using the best our streaming
video services had to offer as a salve. I knew in the
morning I'd have a clearer head and be in a much
better place emotionally to keep the job search going.
I woke up refreshed and determined, and applied for
three jobs before lunchtime.

Adler signed up with Arrangements. I didn't
think she was making a bad choice, just maybe not
the best choice and I wanted her to be safe. Her first
two weeks back in the ring bore very little fruit. A few
dates, a few free meals, but not the big payout
commitment she was looking for.

Those two weeks weren't very successful for
me either. More applications than I could count, only
three callbacks and still no offers.

I felt nauseous as I filled out our next rent
check, all sorts of desperate questions bouncing
around in my head. What was it like to get evicted?
Did I know anyone who would let me stay on their
couch? How long could one sleep in their car?

When I got back from our landlord's drop box,

I asked Adler what her next move was going to be. In doing the mental math, if one of us didn't get a decent paying job in the next three weeks, we were out on our asses. I factored in the two weeks we'd actually have to work to get a check and the two-week's grace our landlord was rumored to give if your situation was really tight.

We had food and I was only using my car to get to and from interviews, but we needed a plan. Better yet, a concrete solution.

"Okay. I know you're going to say no, but Arrangements is having a mixer this weekend. I think you should come."

"Ads, I don't know."

"You have literally nothing to lose. Think of it this way; are you opposed to being a housewife who lets their husband support the family financially?"

"No. I kinda want that actually."

"So imagine you're a housewife, but no kids and you don't have to see your husband every day, and he still pays for everything. And then you may or may not have sex with him."

"I just—"

"What's the fear? What's really bothering you about this?"

"That it means I failed? I got out of North Carolina, got this far, but still couldn't keep it together." Technically becoming a sugar baby was sex work and I had nothing against that. I had friends at home who danced and a college classmate of mine made a killing as a cam girl. But I figured I had to be desperate and past the point of failure to try something I'd be so horribly bad at. I was terrible at faking it.

"Kayla. You didn't fail. You got laid off due to absolutely no fault of your own. I think failure would be giving up and moving back home, which is the last place you want to be." She was right about that part.

"And you don't need to do this forever. Think of it like a heist. Wait no, that's still illegal and you don't like illegal. Think of it as a trip to Vegas—"

"Oh my god, stop. I get it."

"Just try it with me. Come to the mixer and if you meet someone you like then it all works out. If not, we come home and we plan a heist."

"You sure they'll take me? I still don't think I'm the type." The white petite blonde type.

"Trust me. You're someone's type."

"We'll see."

I grabbed my laptop, pulled up the Arrangements website and let Adler comment on every keystroke I made as I set up my profile. "If they reject my application will they email me or will someone come here in person to laugh in my face?"

"Will you shut up!" Alder laughed. "They won't reject you. The very, very worst thing that can happen is that no one…bites."

"No, the worst thing that could happens is that I meet a murderer."

"Whatever. You're almost done. You just need to add a profile picture."

I didn't have any headshots, but I was in a wedding a few month back and was able to crop some of those candids down to pretty spectacular profile pictures. I picked the most flattering option and uploaded it to my profile.

"Okay perfect. Now click on the events tab."

I did and there was only one event listed:

Meet and Mingle
Peak, West Hollywood
Saturday June 20, 2:00pm

"Why is it in the afternoon?" I asked.

"I don't know, actually. The last one I went to was in the afternoon. Maybe so the men can get a look at us in daylight."

"Or maybe any night functions would be past their geriatric bedtime."

"Okay, you cannot say stuff like that."

"I won't. To their faces anyway. Cross my heart."

I clicked the ATTEND button under the details. "Now we wait," Adler said.

"For what? I thought you said I wouldn't be rejected."

"Will you just wait? Let's walk down and get yogurt."

"With what money? We're on a budget, toots," I reminder her.

"Uh... free samples. Duh." Adler jumped up and came back with her flip-flops. I stared at my inbox until she was standing by the door, tapping the jam, waiting for me to get a move on. I bought two bucks worth of yogurt to cover all the "samples" Adler tried.

When we got back there was an email from Monica Lawrence, Arrangements' "Social Manager".

Hi Kayla, Welcome to Arrangements and thank you for RSVPing to our Meet and Mingle. Over forty men from around Southern California will be in town to meet that special someone, someone like you.

"Oh, that's smooth," I muttered.

I call the dress code garden party chic. Light and flirty, but not nightclub. Please feel free to contact me or my associate, Ryan, if you have any questions. Can't wait to meet you. - Monica
Ps. Love your pic. Too cute! :)

"See?" Adler rocked on the couch beside me.
"What if she hadn't loved my pic?"
Adler shrugged. "We'll never know. You're too cute."
"So what do we do now?"
"We shop."
Thanks to my bum roommate I was already two dollars poorer, but this time Adler was onto something. If I was doing this, I was doing it in style.

We both looked cute as hell when we arrived at Peak, Adler in her strapless floral number and me in my tangerine halter maxi dress. The club was smack in the middle of West Hollywood. It boasted a retractable roof that opened over the dance floor and bar area for perfect ventilation while twerking up a sweat. That Saturday afternoon the open ceiling flooded the venue with natural light, bright and inviting.

Monica greeted us at the door. She was extremely tall and bubbly, spray tanned and bleached blonde. I instantly liked her, mostly because she seemed genuine and her laugh was hysterically awkward and infectious. I kinda wanted to hang out by her the whole time, but after she introduced us to Ryan—an effeminate brunette around our age, with only a little less bubble than his associate—Monica practically shoved us into the room.

There were girls. Tons of girls, and a buffet of finger foods and champagne.

"Just smile and be yourself," Adler whispered to me before she swan dove into the first cluster of men we encountered. Being the good friend she was, she pulled me with her, but I was so shocked by how not herself Adler was being I just watched, stunned, after we were all done exchanging names.

Adler was a flirt. I teased her once that she probably winked at the doctor the moment she came out of her mom, but I never knew she could turn it on so good, so strong. The first five guys we met ranged from older, yet moderately attractive, to resurrected forefather, but Adler charmed them all, smiling, touching, giggling, asking all the right questions. I had my own jokes, but as soon as the attention turned to me I found myself clamming up. I wasn't interested in any of these men and, worse, I didn't want any of them to be interested in me.

This went on for most of the afternoon. Adler would try to include me and somehow I'd manage to sweep myself to the side. Yeah, I needed the money, but if this was going to work I was going to need some kind of connection to the man I was going to link myself to.

Eventually I excused myself to go to the restroom and on the way back I hid. The dining area gave you a good view of the dance floor, but it was poorly lit. No one would miss me. I sat down, wishing I'd thought to grab myself a glass of water before I'd made my escape.

"Not your scene?"

"Oh my god!" I almost screamed when I saw the man sitting in the dark booth across from me. How did I miss him? It was dark, but not that dark. My cloud of self-pity must have been pretty thick. Extra thick, 'cause the man was cute. He was a sexy Jesus of sorts, white guy with thick, long black hair past his shoulders, and a thick salt-and-pepper mustache and beard. I couldn't make out the color of his eyes, but he was casually dressed in jeans and a blue or black gingham shirt with the sleeves rolled up. Full lips, all-round nice face. No watch, but he had two cell phones stacked on each other on the table. He was looking over at me.

"I'm sorry." I moved to stand up, trying not to choke on my thudding heart.

"Nah, you're good. Have a seat. Stay awhile."

His voice was kinda sexy too, deep, but with a kindness to it. Inviting. Sincere.

I eased back into the booth. "You sure? I didn't mean to interrupt." Whatever private meeting he was having with the glass in his hand.

"Yeah. It's nice to get away from the crowd."

"You work here?" He had a California bar owner way about him. Maybe he was Monica's contact at Peak, holding the place down so a sugar-coated orgy didn't break out.

"Nah. I'm with the party. Just observing."

"You're a sugar daddy? I mean—sorry."

He shook his head. "You're not wrong. I, uh— I run the company that owns Arrangements."

"Oh." Not what I was expecting.

"Decided to come through, maybe find a nice girl of my own, but nah."

"Not your scene?"

"Not at all, but I figured I'd hang out. Stick around to catch the match-making, watch some love connections spring eternal."

"I gotcha. It's not my scene either."

"Why not just leave?" His eyebrows came together, not in anger, just concern. "You know you don't have to stay or leave with any of these guys."

"Oh no, no. I know. Sorry. My roommate's here too and we drove together. She's gonna find someone for sure. I just want to make sure she gets home okay at this point."

"Did she drag you here?"

"Kind of. I—we both need money. She's been out of work and I just lost my job, and that rent check's due. You know what I mean?"

"I do. I have been there."

"And now you own a sugar daddy website."

"Among other things. So you need money, but this is not your scene."

"I thought I could do it. I'm a people person. I love people. I used to work in human resources before I got let go. I resourced the humans. I can do people, but I thought about it—"

"The sex?"

"Yeah, mostly the sex."

"They don't all want that. Some of these guys just want companionship. Someone who's better at socializing, to make them look good at parties. Someone to take out on the boat."

"I've heard, but the sex is all I can think of. It's what most guys want from me anyway. I mean have you seen this body?" I joked. "I'm a damn fertility goddess."

He didn't laugh outright, but I saw a small smile peek out from under that mustache. "I will not argue with that."

"I just—I need a connection. We don't have to be in love, but I have to like you a little bit. Or at least be attracted to you."

"And none of these guys are working for you."

"No, sir."

"Hmm. But rent's due."

"In three weeks." The tightness came back to my chest. I hoped he couldn't hear it in my voice. "I'm resourceful. I'll think of something."

"We've only been talking for a bit here, but I

don't doubt that for a minute. I'm Michael." He reached across the table and offered his hand. It was warm when I shook it. Warm and dry, but soft.

"Kayla."

"Well Kayla. I know I said I wasn't seeking, but I seem to have found." He reached into his pocket and pulled out a business card. I tried to process what he was getting at as he wrote another number on the blank back.

"If you change your mind about this whole Arrangement arrangement, shoot me a text."

He handed me the card. It just had his full name, Michael Bradbury, and a number on the front in smooth black lettering. It said "personal cell" next to the number on the back.

"Are you even old enough to be a sugar daddy?" I asked.

"Yup. Fifty is right around the corner."

"No way." The beard was graying for sure, but he didn't look a day over forty.

"Trust me. I wouldn't lie about that." He stood and when I looked up I could see that little hint of a smile. It was more in his cheek this time. The slightest hint, but I liked it. It felt honest.

"Text?" I asked.

"I'm in meetings most of the day. I can respond to texts right away. It's hard to tell a business associate to stop talking while I check a voicemail."

I glanced at the card again and somehow found my nerve. "And what if I don't like you enough for the sex?"

"I'm hoping you won't text me unless you do."

And then of course I wanted to jump him.

"Have a good one." He touched my shoulder lightly, and then headed for the door.

Chapter Two

Adler was so proud of me for getting a number she didn't give me any shit for disappearing in the middle of the party and not coming back until I could tell she was ready to leave. Her adventure in Sugar Daddy Land had turned up mixed results. There were a few guys she thought she could work with, but no straight up negotiations had kicked off. I wasn't worried about her though. Now that I'd seen her in action there was no doubt in my mind that she'd find someone soon. Besides, neither of us were looking for Mr. Right or Mr. Forever. She was looking for Mr. 90 Days Max and I was looking for Mr. Hold Me Over Until I Find A Job.

The minute we got home, after picking up some celebratory items off the dollar menu, I Googled Michael Bradbury. He'd undersold himself a little. He didn't just run the company that owned Arrangements. He ran ICO, the mega corporation that owned nearly every popular dating site and app, five media outlets, and FiveStars.com, the most popular consumer opinion site on the planet. He was also on the short list to be the next owner of Los Angeles's NBA franchise. He'd started AskCupid.com with a college buddy and things had just blown up from there.

Michael was forty-nine, he wasn't lying about

that. And, according to his online info, he was single. I went through all the images available, with the charming bonus of Adler's commentary. Most of the pictures were of him court-side at various basketball games, a few pictures of him walking down the street. There was one picture of him in a suit, a fashion shot from an issue of Forbes. The hair was still long and the beard and mustache were still thick, but he cleaned up real well.

His eyes were blue with hints of green.

When I couldn't search anymore, I sat back and sighed. What was I going to do about Michael Bradbury?

"Okay. I'm not gonna pressure you. But. I think. You need. To call him." She said it just like that, all dramatic emphasis.

"He doesn't take calls. All text."

"Then text him," she said, like that business card was burning a hole her pocket.

"And say what?"

"Hey boy. Give me some money?"

"No, but can you be serious for one second."

"Okay. I'm sorry. What do you want to do?"

"I want to text him. He was cool, like really easy to talk to. There was a little flirting, but he didn't come on strong at all. Just matter of fact and cool. Totally my type. And you've seen his face."

"Stone-cold fox. So what's the problem?"

"Okay, I text him. He wants a sugar baby and I want—"

"All the dick you can handle?"

"No. I want a real relationship. Clearly he's

busy and has no time for one or he wouldn't be looking for an arrangement of his own. What if I end up catching all the feelings and all he can give me is one weekend a month?"

"And spending money."

"And that."

"And what if you met at a bar. A different bar, and he just worked in an office and you liked him, but he wasn't giving you the time you wanted 'cause he was too busy hanging with his friends? Or because he had another girl on the side? Or his mom hated you? Do you see what I'm getting at here? Any guy can break your heart. Any guy."

"Ugh, you're right."

"I say text him, but be up front. Tell him that feelings are a thing for you."

"He knows that."

"You told him that?"

"It was like the first thing out of my mouth and then he gave me his card. After he kinda hinted that if we got together sex would definitely be on the table."

Adler grabbed my arm and almost pulled it out of the socket. "Kaaaaylaaaaa! Text him right now!"

My laughed was a little rattled. "No."

"He knows you're a big softy and he's okay with that, and you know that he wants to dump his cum on you and you're okay with that."

"Am I though? Am I really? With the cum dumping?"

"Yes. You two are practically engaged. But all jizzing aside, he's clearly a smart guy who makes great business decisions. If he didn't want to see you again he wouldn't have given you his personal cell number."

Adler had me there. There was no doubt in my mind that Michael was at least a little bit interested in me. I knew I kind of owed it to the universe to give him a call. Or a text. I wanted to wait at least a few days. Four hours would make me feel a little desperate.

"And don't even think about waiting three days or whatever stupid dating rules I know you live by. I don't think he's gonna hook up with someone else right away, but he's definitely not gonna play games. The good ones don't. If you want him, text him. Tonight."

"Fine. I'm going to get changed. We're going to watch the best Saturday night TV movie cable has to offer and, sometime before I go to bed, I will text him and let him know I am interested in getting to know him better."

"Good. And I'm going to email Ronald Leinhertz and ask him if his hip is good enough for golf tomorrow."

"The old, old guy?"

"Oh the oldest."

"Well good luck with that."

My night went exactly as planned. In my pajamas on the couch watching a teen pregnancy somehow turn into a double murder-suicide. Adler hassled me about texting Michael for a good hour, but once she was distracted by the shiny things the internet had to offer I snuck and sent Michael a text.

Or two.

Still on the fence about an "arrangement".
But I am interested.
In you.

I put my phone on vibrate on the off-chance he actually texted me back. I didn't want to alert the fiend on the other end of the couch.

His response time was less than two minutes.

At a fundraiser right now.
What's your day like tomorrow?

I did my best to hide my smile as I texted him back. Adler was something of a smile detective. She could sniff out guy-related giddiness at fifty paces.

Free. Free Monday too. And Tuesday. Still unemployed. Free forever.

Hopefully he thought I was as funny as I did. Again, a response in less than two minutes.

You'll hear from me tomorrow. And maybe you'll be with me on Monday. And Tuesday. Maybe forever.

I covered my mouth and managed not to squeal loud enough for Michael to hear me across town. But, of course, I played it cool.

I don't hate that idea. Talk soon. Night.

The text bubbles were bubbling before I even hit send.

Goodnight Kayla.

Adler couldn't tell from where she was sitting, but I actually died. My ghost was floating somewhere above the couch, squeeing at the top of her lungs.

Adler was gone when I woke up on Sunday morning. Probably out hiking with her friend, Sienna, or at brunch with Sienna, spending money she didn't have. I made the cheapest breakfast I could make—let's hear it for eggs—then went for a walk of my own. I read on a blog that it's good to get out of the house when you're unemployed. Keeps the mood slumps away, or from getting worse.

I sent up another prayer of thanks for our in-unit washer and dryer, thankful as hell that I didn't have to drag my ass to a crowded laundromat on Sunday. The job boards were waiting for me, but I couldn't focus. I wanted to hear from Michael. So I cleaned and cleaned and then organized and cleaned some more.

When Adler came back I realized how tense I'd been. I was too happy to see her, like it was Michael coming through the door. I knew then that I was already banking too much on this non-existent relationship. It wasn't even the money. It was the emotional distraction of it all. The idea of just hearing from Michael made me so happy it took my mind off the painful horror of applying for every HR position I could find. That realization was all I needed to get my butt back in front of my laptop.

Adler brought enough dinner leftovers for us both and swore up and down that Sienna wouldn't let her pay.

"Hey your phone is ringing!" She called to me while I was waiting for the microwave to chime. "It's him! It's him!" She ran into the kitchen and practically threw my phone at me. Sure 'nuff Michael Bradbury's name lit up my screen.

"Hello?" You could hear how nervous I was.

"Hi. Did I get you at a bad time?"

"Nope. Still unemployed. Still massively not sure how I feel about this."

"Can I swing by and pick you up? I have to fly to New York tonight, but I thought we could talk on my way to the airport. My driver will bring you home."

"Oh, um yeah. I'll text you my address."

"Sounds good. I'll see you soon."

"'K, bye."

I threw my phone back at Adler and ran to my room. I had to de-hobo.

"He's coming to pick me up so we can talk."

"What did he say?!" Adler stood in my doorway asking me stupid questions for thirty seconds before she realized this was not a fucking game and I needed to get ready. "I got outfit. You do make-up and hair."

I was sweating by the time I pulled it together, but when Michael called to say he was outside, I looked effortlessly fabulous, yet Sunday relaxed. Tight ripped jeans that highlighted my curvaceous thighs and my oversized white top that dipped low in the back showing off the new-ish black lace bra I had on. Some black wedges and I was power walking for the elevator.

A shiny black Suburban was waiting right there at the curb. The driver came around the side and opened the door for me. Michael was inside, but he wasn't alone. I tried not to look disappointed as I climbed in. His hint of a smile took care of that though.

He leaned over and brushed my cheek with his soft lips. "Hey," he said quietly.

"Hi."

We started moving. Michael gestured to the guy sitting in the row behind us. "This is my assistant, Ruben."

Ruben was a very tiny white guy with a shaved head and the sweetest smile. He reached forward and shook my hand. "Love the top."

"Thank you."

"So," Michael glanced at his phone, checking the time. He did have a flight to catch. "Let's discuss this. In the strictest terms, you would be a girlfriend for hire. What does that mean to you?"

"Wait. You have to back up. I have questions."

"Good. I'm glad to hear that. Shoot."

"One, why are you single?" I turned around and glanced at Ruben. "Are you just consumed by your career or are you really an asshole in disguise?"

"Huge asshole," Ruben said, but there was a cheeky smile.

"I've dated, plenty, but I have been consumed with work."

"So why now? Why me?"

"I think you touched on something important when we met. I've dated a lot, but no one has really brought that something special to the table that made me think a relationship was worth pursuing. I've had fun but, as you said, I have to feel something."

"You want to pursue a relationship with me? You feel something with me?" I asked, trying to ignore the irrational romantic in my head that was running around in circles, screaming.

"I do. I think you're beautiful and you appear to be honest and upfront. All things that I think are very important."

I shifted on the seat so I was facing him. "And in your forty-nine years, you've never met a girl who fit that criteria?"

A little smirk appeared on his lips. "I have, but timing matters too. On both our parts."

"So you feel good about this timing?"

"For myself, I do. Yes. And you?"

"I am unemployed. And there have been people before, but the timing was off. We'll go with that." I chewed my lip, trying to think of what else I wanted to say. He was making sense, I still wasn't sure. I didn't love the sound of girlfriend-for-hire. Michael waited patiently. "Honestly, I don't know. I've never done this before so I have no idea how it works and I don't know if it would work for me."

"Then I'll start with what it means to me. I will take care of you financially, handle any bills you have and give you what is essentially an allowance. We will spend any free time we choose to together and you have the option to accompany me to any of the many social events I need to show my face at. It's the same thing I would do with any girlfriend, but you're in a financial bind that I know of up front and I want to help."

"Okay. Okay. Is there anything else?"

"You're still wondering about the sex?"

"Ah yeah."

"I didn't forget the rest of our conversation. I'm attracted to you and I would hope that you're attracted to me."

"I am."

"I wouldn't want any woman to sleep with me out of any obligation, financial or otherwise. Let's say my door is open and if you ever find yourself wanting to cross that threshold..."

"Okay. Still not sure though."

"She's smart," Ruben said with a laugh. "Don't give in to his shit, Kayla. Make him negotiate."

I couldn't help but laugh a little myself. "I'm not trying to drive a hard bargain. I just have reservations. This is a little weird to me. Fine, I'm just gonna ask the one thing I know I shouldn't, but it'll kill me if I don't. Are you looking for fun or are you looking to settle down? I know we're talking about a sugar arrangement, but I would like to know where you're really coming from."

"Yes, girl," Ruben hissed under his breath.

Michael glared at his assistant for a fraction of a second before he answered. "I'll be honest and say that I am looking to settle down. I had never intended to be single this long."

"Thank you. I just—I just needed to know if this position is... part-time temporary. Or part-time with room for growth."

"How about a date?" Michael suggested just as we pulled into the airport. I'd been to LAX dozens of times, but I'd never been in through this way. Their driver pulled us out onto the runway, onto a private tarmac where a smooth, clean jet was waiting. We were out of time. I should probably make a decision.

"I can do a date."

"We'll go on a regular date and if you feel like you want to keep seeing me we'll discuss how I can assist you financially. I'd at least like to help you out until you get back on your feet."

"That's very kind of you, thank you. Do you want to just call me when you get back from New York?"

"I was thinking you'd come with me."

"To New York? I guess I could, but I—"

"I'll only be there two days, but I'm shoving a lot into this trip so you'll get a taste of what it's like to be with me and I'll get a chance to see what it's like to be with you."

"But I didn't bring anything to wear." I had my wallet, my phone, and the clothes on my back.

"I have a shopper in the city. Just give Ruben your sizes and he'll take care of it."

"I—yeah. Sure. Why not." Under any other circumstances I would say no. We'd basically just met, but Michael was on to something. Getting to know each other a bit before I made my decision was a great idea.

Also there was one thing that made running off with him different than disappearing for a few days with a random guy I'd met at work or online. Michael was super rich, and Adler knew his name. He wouldn't be hard to find if I came up missing or floating in the Hudson. Besides, a little adventure was just what the unemployment doctor ordered.

"Let me just tell my roommate." I climbed out of the SUV and shot off the most frantic text of my life as I followed Michael to the jet.

Going to NYC with Michael for a few days. If you don't hear from me in eight hours I've been murdered. Tell my mom. Then avenge me.

"Ready?" I looked up as Michael's hand landed lightly on the small of my back.

"Yeah," I said, trying to breathe.

I had first-day-of-school-in-a-fancy-museum-where-everything-is-breakable-and-really-expensive jitters. We got settled on the plane, on a plush sectional that ran up the right side of the cabin. There was a gorgeous table and two massive recliners on the left side. Farther back there were four more recliners facing a wide screen TV hung on the rear wall. There was more beyond that, maybe the restroom, the maid's quarters. A pony stable.

Michael and I sat on the sectional. Before Ruben took his seat he handed me a tablet and a stylus. I looked at the document on the screen and asked the obvious question. The words Non-disclosure Agreement were printed clearly at the top, but I had no idea why he was handing it to me.

"I need to sign a NDA to date you?"

"No, for Michael's business," Ruben said.

"While we're in the City you'll be privy to a lot of face to face meetings and business calls," Michael said. "I need to know that everything you hear or see will be kept in confidence. You can talk about us to whomever you like, but I have to protect the business."

"Oh, okay."

"And I have to let you know that we might be photographed. I haven't been on a date in a while. It won't hit TMZ levels of madness, but some paps will take interest."

"He's so boring in public though. If you match that level of blah, they'll get bored of you both in like a minute," Ruben teased.

"I can handle that," I said, but mentally I

paused. I'd have to tell my mom something if I decided to take this all the way. She loved grocery tabloids. She did not need to find out about Michael and my potential relationship that way.

As the crew readied for take off Michael walked me through every section of the document. He was sitting so close, almost leaning into me as we went over each part. I didn't fight the way my body reacted to him, but I think I hid my lust for him pretty well. He just smelled so good, like some cologne they only sold in stores I'd never be rich enough to shop in. And I loved his voice. I wanted him closer, touching me, but we were taking this slowly. On his private jet. To spend two nights together. Three thousand miles away from home.

I ignored the oddness of the situation and focused on the task in front of us. The NDA was short, but thorough and firm. I wasn't to blab about anything I heard. Period. I signed the bottom line and handed the tablet back to Ruben.

Michael sat back as the flight attendant came around and greeted us, letting us know we'd be taking off soon. I wanted to relax, but I was afraid I would screw something up. I didn't know what there was for me to screw up. All I had to do was sit there and not try to crash the plane, but I was nervous. Michael was sitting next to me, leaning against the plush fabric of the sectional, his long legs stretched out in front of him, ankles crossed. He had on a pristine pair of white Converse. He looked like he was settling in for a good nap, but then Ruben started talking.

"You have Johnson at 9:00. That's going to run

long," Ruben said, as another of the flight attendants appeared with fancy bottles of water. She was a gorgeous brunette, maybe in her forties. She had kind eyes.

"The gentlemen will have their usual, but can I get you anything to drink?"

"A ginger ale if you have it."

"We sure do. And I can put your bag up as well."

"Oh thank you. What's your name?" I asked.

"Sandy."

"Thank you, Sandy. Kayla." I grabbed my phone and handed her my purse, which didn't quite match our mode of transportation. She popped a small panel on the wall that opened to a shallow cabinet, storing my stuff safely on a shelf. I was actually impressed by a hidden shelf.

"We'll eat after takeoff," Michael said. "I still eat like a college student. Chicken tenders okay?"

"Yeah sure." I didn't want to tell him that I was more than accustomed to eating like a *poor* college student.

"So you have Johnson at 9:00," Ruben said again. Of course, they had business. I supposed I could busy myself on my phone. It had already linked to the plane's Wi-Fi, but I didn't know if that was the right thing to do. I didn't want to be rude, so I just waited patiently, taking turns studying Ruben and his mannerisms, and every visible inch of Michael's body. And his voice. The things Ruben said that made him laugh. The things Ruben said that annoyed him. Not that Ruben said them, but the messages that were being delivered.

Michael's trip to NYC was pretty packed. I knew he said he wanted to spend more time with me, but I had no idea how he was going to manage that. Meetings all morning, a lunch meeting, an appointment in the afternoon followed by a dinner meeting. The next day sounded like it was mapped out the same. Meeting, meeting, meeting with a meal, meeting, and then back on this flying mansion to return to LA. I'm sure the rest of his week was the same.

We took off and, like Michael said, dinner was served the moment we were in the air. While we ate they continued to talk schedules, and what Michael wanted out of this trip and what he wanted to put into it. For example, someone named Richard Arnold was a hair away from getting fired. And then someone named Alice Crammer was up for a review. Michael was proud of her work, but he wanted to meet with her in person so they could touch bases. There was an apartment he was thinking about looking at, but that was less of a priority. By the time Sandy brought dessert I saw the obvious need for the NDA. Michael and Ruben talked about *everything*.

Listening to them talk helped me relax too. The focus was completely off me and I could just observe. Until Michael turned to me and, as he touched my hand, said the last thing I expected to hear from a man like him. "One thing you should know about me, I'm a bit on the affectionate side. Is that cool?"

"Yeah. Thank you for asking." I swallowed the nerves in my throat. I touched him back, letting him play with my fingers and my palm while he continued to talk business with Ruben. I tried to ignore the butterflies that were dancing in my stomach and my underwear. It didn't work though. I was so fucked.

After a bit, he turned to me again. "We have about five hours 'til we land. I haven't slept a full eight hours since before college, but I like to catch a few hours of shuteye on these longer jaunts. You want to join me?" He nodded past the TV, toward the pony stables.

"Uh, sure."

Ruben wouldn't let me leave until I gave him my sizes, including my bra, underwear and shoe size. Since we were getting personal I asked him for a satin scarf as well. I could get through a few hours without it on a plane, but I wasn't going three nights without wrapping my hair. After Ruben got all the relevant information out of me, Michael reached out for my hand again. He led me into a large room in the back of the plane, complete with a gigantic bed.

Chapter Three

"I've never slept in the thing," Michael said nodding toward the bed of the gods. "I usually just nap on top of the sheets."

"A napper?"

"Yep. I get what sleep I can here and there. Most of the time in chairs."

"And on top of sheets."

"Yep. And I bet you're the all the way in type. All the way under the covers. You're a snuggler."

"Oh totally. You should see my bed. It's ridiculous. Tons of pillows and I have a down comforter and this fluffy fleece blanket. I even got this silly teddy bear that doubles as a pillow. Pure fluff."

"I get that about you. Well, this will have to do for now. We'll have to get you fluffed up later."

I didn't know whether he was joking or not. The bed had mountains of pillows and a suede comforter. If I didn't want to spend the whole flight talking to him and hoping he'd touch me in my pants I'd burrow right into the thing and be out like a light.

I took the lead and climbed onto the bed with my clothes on, kicking off my shoes as I went. Michael joined me, but he kept his shoes on.

We looked at each other, I think for the first time. He was so good looking that I knew I'd been looking around him, or just in his general direction. I'd taken good stock of his hands, how long his legs were, and shape of his thighs before dinner, but his face? Whew. His face. It was pretty.

He wanted to touch me some more, I think, but we were both being shy. Or careful. I knew if I made the first move something weird would happen, like I'd go right for his crotch and I'm talking over the jeans. Just grab the whole thing in my palm and then stare at him like it was the sexiest, most normal thing in the world. Or apologize profusely while still holding fast, or squeezing harder. The whole thing played out in my head and I laughed, just buried my face in the soft covers and laughed, which was just as embarrassing as grabbing his dick.

"What?" he asked, before he gave my shoulder a gentle shake. "Whaatt?"

"You're so hot. Do you know that?"

"I feel like I look homeless half the time, but okay."

"No." I reached up and touched his beard. "It's so hot."

"I'll take your word for it. So human resources."

"Ugh, yeah." I flopped onto my back and looked up at the tiny lights embedded in the ceiling. It was easier to complain without looking at a ridiculously hot man. Hot men threw your whole perspective out of alignment. "It was fine. It paid well enough, loved my coworkers—"

"But not the dream."

"Not even close."

"Or what you went to school for."

"Ha, no. I don't even know what I went to school for. I got a degree in Political Science and that's only because I was undecided forever, but I'd bonded with one of my professors. She was like the grandma I never had, so I just kept taking her courses. By the time I had to declare I had accidentally set my course track."

"So no political office for you. No political consulting."

"No."

"What is for you then, Kayla Davis?"

I looked over at him. His eyes were so blue and they were focused right on my lips. I had to look back at the ceiling. It was impossible to talk to him like that. "I was thinking about graphic design, and digital art, and I kind of want to learn to code. I know I'm only twenty-four, but I feel so far behind. I'll find the coolest stuff online, like a photorealistic painting of Lucy Liu done in Illustrator and like a fifteen year old drew it. I'd be dead before I caught up."

"Well you'd need to start somewhere. Seems like the art is important."

"I love to draw and if I could translate that skill to a digital medium, maybe someone would pay me to do it full time. Right now I'm still in the colored pencils/crayon phase."

"And the coding?"

"As you know, every company has a need for it. I'd learn a valuable skill. But it's kind of hard to find the motivation to start when you get tanked from a job you don't even really want, but you still have rent to pay."

I thought Michael was going to offer me money again, but he didn't. "It is tough when things are going in one direction, but you want to focus on another. I want to touch you," he said kind of out of the blue, but not at all because it was exactly what I was thinking.

"I want you to, but also, there's touching hands and then there's—"

"The fact that we're on our first date. Don't want to rush it."

I licked my lips. "Yeah."

"Then we won't. Tell me more about you."

It was work to tell my vagina she would have to wait, but I managed to get my lust under control and just talk. I told him about myself, my kind of conservative parents and my baby sisters, our place in Nowhere, North Carolina. He had a younger sister too and a younger brother. They grew up poor in Michigan.

He'd earned a scholarship that had led him to the college roommate that helped him make his first million. His parents were still around, but his mom was showing early signs of dementia. I appreciated him sharing that bit with me. I could tell he loved his mom but, I don't know, the way he told me just made me want to know more about him. It didn't dampen the mood.

He mentioned what was next for him. The NBA deal was real, but he was on the fence. Owning a franchise was a dream of his, a dream of most basketball fans. He knew that would take precedence over all his other ventures and he wasn't sure if he was ready to let the world of online dating go.

We talked until the plane landed. So much for a nap. I was fine until about halfway to the city. The lack of sleep kicked me in the ass. My eyes were blinking closed when we pulled up to this fancy Manhattan hotel. Michael guided me through the lobby and I shamelessly rested against his shoulder as Ruben checked us in. I heard the woman behind the desk joke that they needed to hurry and get me off to bed. I must have muttered something, because they all had a good laugh.

Michael got me upstairs to a room I apparently had to myself. Ruben was a floor below and Michael was next door to me. We'd spend the night together if and when I was ready, he said quietly, as I zombie walked to another massive bed. I was climbing into this one for sure. But before I could, Michael's arms were around me. It was so dangerous. My whole body melted against him. He felt so good. Warm and sturdy.

And then he kissed me. It was quick, kind of, or just not as long as I wanted it to be. But it was perfect and completely first date appropriate. That mustache tickled my face like crazy, but his lips were so soft. When he pulled away his lips brushed against my cheek and my neck. My neck, over and over. I pressed my pelvis against him. As soon as I could keep my eyes open, it was on.

"When we get back to L.A., okay? When you decide," he whispered.

"Okay." I managed to get out.

"Do you want me to stay with you for a while?"

I nodded. "Yeah." I was dead tired, but I didn't want him to leave. Not yet.

"Okay. In you go." Michael pulled back the blankets while I kicked my shoes off. I ditched my jeans and my bra, leaving on my drawers and my drop back shirt. I really needed some clothes. I was afraid Michael had seen what gravity does to double D's and was about to make a break for it when he didn't join me under the covers. He tucked me in instead then climbed on top of the bed and spooned me.

"No skin-to-skin until L.A. too?" I mumbled.

"Not unless you want it to end with dick in pussy? Or dick in ass?" He gave my butt a little pat.

I think I laughed. Or maybe I just fell asleep.

The trip to New York was weird, but good. Michael was busy. Very busy. But when he was tied up I hung out with Ruben. Michael was already in his second meeting when I finally woke up. My phone had magically found its way onto a proper charger and there were a series of texts leaving me all sorts of crucial information, like Michael's and Ruben's room numbers, which I'd totally missed while I'd been sleepwalking, and Ruben's cell number.

I sent him a text letting him know I was up and, not ten minutes later, he and a nice girl named Angelique brought me new clothes and a toothbrush.

And the perfect satin scarf, bless her heart. Once I showered and changed, I answered the seven hundred texts from Adler letting her know the name of the hotel where we were staying and when we'd be back. Then we got lunch.

Angelique had to get back to her job at Teen Vogue after we ate. As he paid the bill, Ruben let me know the driver was taking us to pick up Michael for his appointment. I was so anxious to see him and continue with our date, but I was worried about the nature of his appointment. Was Michael sick? What if he'd come all the way to New York so he could see a specialist? I wanted to ask him as soon as he hopped in the SUV, but we weren't there yet. It was too early in our arrangement to be digging for those details. He put me partially at ease when he kissed me, almost on sight. It felt natural. It felt like he'd been anxious to see me too.

And you don't even have to imagine my relief when we pulled up to a barbershop in Harlem. I almost lost it when all the men in attendance cheered for "White Mike" when he came in the door. He laughed the nickname off and hopped right in the chair for a straight razor shape-up.

Oh they had some jokes for me too, asking what I was doing with his old ass, saying they knew he was going to end up with a sistah, just not one so thick. They appreciated his taste. All good-natured cracks. I couldn't stop laughing and blushing like an idiot. It reminded of me of going to the barbershop with my dad and my uncle.

When they weren't teasing us I couldn't keep

my eyes off Michael. He came right over to me as soon as he was done.

"How do I look?" he asked. His barber had managed to preserve the perfect thickness of his beard and mustache while cleaning up his neck and clearing all the errant hairs in his mustache. He looked good before, but a great barber could, well...

"You took him from an A to an A+." I looked at Julius and winked.

A chorus of "Ah shits!" and "Okay, Jules!" erupted around the room. There were a few more minutes of conversation. Michael made a loose appointment for the following month, then led me out the door.

That night we had dinner with a rep from the NBA. That conversation was interesting. He versed Michael in the full details of what his role as owner would be if he decided to purchase a team. He had to be part nurturing, yet stern, father, part party promoter, while dealing with the variety of personalities and families on an NBA roster.

The whole time he was touching me, a hand in my lap or an arm around my shoulder. He checked in with me often, making sure I wasn't bored to death, and each time he punctuated his concern with a kiss to my cheek or my temple. The whole thing was actually pretty interesting. I tried to just listen, but I had some questions about things like the draft process and dealing with players that have run-ins with the law. I apologized on reflex for interrupting, but Michael and Mr. Sands seemed happy with the directions my questions took the conversation.

When Mr. Sands excused himself to go to the restroom, I got a real proper kiss right on the lips. The affection was working for me. I already liked Michael. He was easy to talk to, calm and sweet. And he was honest. Everything he'd talked about with Ruben on the plane was repeated to Mr. Sands with equal frankness. I liked that, but the way he was touching me made me like him even more. I was starting to feel like I was his, as if maybe when we got back to L.A. we'd be able to work something out.

We were out pretty late, but when it was clear I was fading. Michael excused us and took me back to the hotel. We only kissed again before I changed for bed, but he stayed with me again until I fell asleep. He didn't question my satin scarf.

The next day was more of the same. Ruben took me shopping in the morning, but I only bought a few things. A new handbag and a wallet to match. I was almost sick at the price tags, but he insisted that Michael had asked him to buy me things and coming back empty handed was not an option.

We grabbed a quick bite then checked out of the hotel and picked up Michael and headed for the airport. This trip only generated more discussions and more meetings to prep for, so, once we were in the air, I stretched out with my head in Michael's lap and dozed most of the way home. He rubbed my side the whole time.

When we landed Michael was quiet. I followed him off the plane to a waiting Suburban, but before we got in he turned to me.

"I think this is the end of our date. If you want it to end, that is."

"And if I don't?"

"You could come back to my house."

"And we could do the sex?"

"If you want to. We could also have some food and watch a movie."

I sucked on my lower lip and looked down at my new wedge heels between us. They matched my new bag. This new thing between us would be more than sex. It would be sex and dinners and meetings. And time. And money. So many lectures from my mom about doing for myself bounced around my head. Lectures about never owing anyone money, how money was a good way to let people control me. But I didn't feel like Michael was trying to control anything. He was just offering something I needed and a few other things I really, really wanted.

I looked up into his blue eyes and was put at ease by what I saw. No pressure, just genuine interest. He could let me go right now, if that was what I wanted, but he was interested in keeping me around a little longer. I wanted to keep him around too.

"Let's go to your place. I want to see how good you are at the sex. And then I'll make my final decision."

"Yes, girl!" I heard Ruben yell from the steps of the plane. His outburst melted the look of shock right off Michael's face as we both laughed.

When we got in the car, I texted Adler again to let her know I'd be out another night. We dropped Ruben off at his boyfriend's place in Santa Monica then got on the PCH. As we went by the Topanga Pass I realized where we were heading, but I didn't say anything. Just moved closer to Michael on the seat.

We were both in our heads I think. It's strange when you know for sure that you're going to have sex. Or when you know you're waiting to have sex. I wasn't worried about it being good. Michael already knew how to touch me and he sure as hell knew how to kiss. There was a chance he was into some freaky shit I couldn't get down with, but I doubted that too. It was clear that the Michael you saw was the Michael you got and, so far, what I saw didn't send up any creeper alarms.

We pulled up a winding hill in one of those fancy Malibu neighborhoods I'd only heard of. Michael's place was at the back of a massive cul-de-sac that only housed two other lots. Each was different, with a different high fence to hide the wealth from neighbors and lost delivery drivers. We went through a set of tall gates that opened to a wide driveway with a bit of an incline. The house was gorgeous, relatively new looking, white with tons of glass, and I could see even from the front that it looked out over a hidden valley and possibly the ocean beyond that.

But I didn't really care about the house. His driver, PJ, drove us straight into the garage and, after getting out of the vehicle, I followed Michael through a side door into a mud room on one side of the living room. Some of the lights were already on. A long hallway, and we were in his bedroom. He flicked a switch and only a bit of dim illumination guided the way to his bed. Another massive bed. I'd have to have Adler and at least seven other friends over for a sleepover some time.

This silence between us was working. We both knew we didn't need to say a word. I just wanted him to kiss me. When he did I realized the kisses we'd shared so far were tame. Child's play. Those kisses were his way of testing the waters and showing me how badly he wanted me close by. This kiss? It made me want him inside of me, like now. Faster than now. My pussy was done waiting. That was clear by how wet I was and the almost painful way my muscles were clenching and releasing. My body needed something to hold on to. When he pulled away for just a second, my breath was all short and quick.

I pretended not to think it was a little funny when he produced a hair tie out of nowhere and pulled back his hair. I'd tease him about it another time.

He kissed me again and, this time, his hands went to the button on my jeans. I went for the buttons on his shirt, but he shook his head slightly.

"I got that."

"I want to touch you."

"You will, but if I don't go down on you soon—"

"What'll happen?" I asked, even though I didn't stop him from pulling down my zipper.

"I'll wait longer until you let me go down on you."

"I'm not going to do that to either of us."

"Good." He pulled down my pants and I stepped out of them, but he left my underwear on. It was one of the pairs Angelique picked out for me, black cotton boy shorts that practically turn into a thong on an ass like mine.

Michael seemed to like them. My eyes were closed, but I could tell by the way he let the word "Fuck" slip out of his mouth as he gave my ass a full manual inspection. His right hand found its way around to my front and it was my turn to bite out a "Fuck" or two.

I was already so wet and swollen I wanted to fall onto the bed when he found my clit through the layer of cotton. He rubbed me with just the tips of his fingers for a while and I had to use his body to hold myself up.

Then his whole hand got involved. I had to open my legs a bit more so he could work with the thickness of my thighs, but it was not a problem. He was rubbing me roughly, the heel of his hand grinding against my clit. He moved the soaked strip of cotton just out of the way and his perfect fingers were inside me. He'd said something about going down on me, but I knew I was going to come just like that, right on his hand.

He pulled me closer and I held onto him, praying my legs wouldn't give out. I came, on my tiptoes, practically sobbing against his shoulder. He lowered me to the bed, where I tried to come back to myself, but my thighs were still shaking and breathing was tough.

When I opened my eyes he was getting undressed. I didn't know when he found the time, but he worked out. Michael wasn't bulky. Still, even before he peeled off his undershirt, I could tell he was cut. He liked ink too. A large piece covered his left pec and shoulder and later, when I gave him a full once-over, I was pretty sure I would find it extended to his back. Boxer briefs were the choice, for tonight at least, but I was more concerned about what was under them.

He was hard. I'd felt it against my stomach the moment we started kissing. And he was perfect; good length, excellent girth, perfect combo of craftsmanship on the circumcision and genes. He reached for a condom in his nightstand. I held my hand out for it. I would get it on there before we got to the big show, but I wanted him in my mouth first.

I sat up and motioned for him to come closer. I supposed I could've gone all porn star with it and licked the tip for forty-five minutes, but I was not about that. I sucked him good and slow, taking as much of him into my mouth as I could. I used my hand for the rest. I tasted his precum on my tongue. That triggered something and I needed him in me right then and there. Condom on and then I slid back farther on the bed, stripping off my bra and my blouse and my ruined underwear as I went. He seemed pleased with what he saw.

He felt right on top of me, and even better when he slowly pushed himself inside. I knew I was tight and we both needed a second, but just a second. I asked him for more. He gave me what I wanted, kissing me as he ground his way deeper.

Michael's stroke game was on point, not the jackhammering I'd experienced before. I liked it deep and powerful, the way he was giving to me. I didn't have to beg, but I did, over and over, begging him not to stop even though tiny orgasms were already erupting inside me. He came before I finished, pressing his face into my hair as he let out the sexiest groan I'd ever heard. But when I expected him to pull out, he found some reserve of strength, a renewable energy source, and kept going. It was not even the perfect way he was fucking me, but the idea that, even when this man was finished, he wasn't gonna stop until I couldn't move anymore.

That made me climax, thinking about him and his freakish level of determination when it came to me and my pussy. I came hard, arching against him. I was disappointed when he climbed off me because it was one of those tricky orgasms that didn't tire me out, it just made me want to go for the rest of the night. But this was Michael Bradbury and he didn't get this far in life by packing it in early.

He shuffled down the bed, pausing for a minute to remind me and my nipples that he hadn't forgotten about them, and then I felt his tongue and his lips and the roughness of his beard pressed against my entrance. That was it. That was how I died. Kayla Davis, age twenty-four. Cause of death: Sexed into oblivion by one Michael Bradbury, Internet billionaire and master of cunnilingus.

Chapter Four

I should have known Michael wouldn't sleep for long, or even close to the whole night. I was up with the sun, which is kind of a given in a house that is practically made of glass. I didn't mind though. I hadn't slept much, but after the second time Michael and I proved our physical compatibility, I conked out and I slept hard. When I opened my eyes Michael was gone from the bedroom, but I could hear him, outside the room somewhere, maybe down the hall, talking on the phone. Business, of course. It was still the workweek and I supposed his associates in New York were three hours ahead and already on the job.

I was still naked. There was the option of throwing on my clothes from the day before, but I couldn't resist the ol' it's-sexy-to-wrap-yourself-in-the-top-sheet gag. This might work with a twin sheet, but I was working with a Cal King. Michael came in as I was trying to untangle it from the blanket and the far corner of the bed. So much for sexy. I had wrapped the length of my body exactly once, with about three times to go when I looked up and saw him smiling that smile that loved to hide underneath his scruff.

I froze as he came toward me, then straightened up and had the good sense to pout for help. I pointed to the corner of the bed.

"If Larchmount is serious, then he needs to bring something serious to the table. I've talked to Steven about it already." He leaned forward and freed the corner and then he came closer to me. I thought he was going to help me finish the job. No. "If we're going to invest, they need to scale back." He looped his fingers on the white fabric covering my boobs and pulled it down to my waist. "Exactly. They aren't trying to start an app. They're trying to start five apps under one umbrella." He gently used his knuckle to brush one nipple and then the other. "I need to know they can handle one step before I give them money to take five." He leaned forward and kissed one of my nipples and then the other. I couldn't keep my eyes open.

He straightened back up, but kept his hands on my body. An arm came around my waist and pulled me closer. His hand slid down to my butt. "Let's go down and see them on Friday. Maybe we can help them find their focus. Yeah, okay. Thanks, bye." He ended his call and tossed his phone into the middle of bed. I looked at his perfect lips as his other arm came around my waist.

"I'm going into the office in a little while. Do you want to stay here or do you want a ride back to your place?"

I want to stay with you, I almost said, completely horrified by how crazy that would sound. But I was already that sprung. And I hadn't even come to a decision yet. "Um, I'll take a ride. It'll be kinda weird to be here alone all day."

"Well you wouldn't be alone. Holger is out in

the guest house."

"Holger?"

"My chef/housekeeper/assassin for hire."

"Oh, you have an Alfred?"

"I do. He keeps an eye on things."

"Holger sounds great, but I think I should head home. Check on my roommate. Show my face so she knows you didn't murderer me."

"Murderer you?"

"Long story. Just let me throw something on and we can go." I turned to find my new overnight bag, but he gently pulled me back.

"Slow down. It's still pretty early."

"I know, but you're up this early making business calls. I figured the office was waiting for you."

"We have time."

"For what?"

He didn't tell me. He just kissed me deep and slow. And then he pulled the sheet all the way off.

Thanks to L.A. traffic, my apartment was a cool hour out of the way from where Michael's office sat in Westwood. I wanted to feel bad about it, but the stop and go meant I got to spend more time with him so I didn't complain. It also gave me more time to think about what the hell I was going to do. I was still in my post-sex haze, completely comfortable with the quiet between us as we made our way down the PCH and back into town. I didn't want this first date to be our last.

Michael took one short call on the fancy Bluetooth feature in his Mercedes G-Class and the rest of the time he sang along with almost every song on the 90s satellite station. He had a terrible voice, but the enthusiasm made it cute. When we got closer to my place I asked the obvious question.

I looked down at our fingers, toying together on my thigh, before I looked up at his profile. "So I got to see what it's like to be around you. How do you feel about being around me?"

"I like being around you."

"But... why me? This isn't insecurity, I swear. You're just, you're paying right? So why not pay for—"

"A prostitute."

"Well yeah, I get it, you own dating sites. Those who can't do, teach. Or start an app. I just want to know where you're coming from, where your head's really at."

"Remember before we left and we talked about relationships? Prostitutes don't do relationships with Johns," he said with a smirk, but the light lift of lips quickly dropped. "Even I see there was a conflict of interest with me showing up at the sugar social."

"Okay. That's fair. I—"

"You're normal."

The frankness of his tone caught me off guard. He went on before I could ask him to explain.

"My life is not normal. I don't do normal

things, so it's hard for me to just run into a normal girl in a Starbucks. I like normal. I miss normal, but the money attracts certain kinds of people. Men and women. And the money attracts a kind of person that isn't always good for *me*. When I look at you, I see a normal, gorgeous girl with a good head on her shoulders and a good heart. You're funny."

"I am. Go on."

He laughed. "And you think. When I asked you to come to New York with me, I know you thought about exactly what you were doing before you got on that plane. Most women I've met would have just called all their friends and told them to come along so they could party on my dime."

"Yeah. That's not me."

"I know it's not. But that's why I'd like to spend more time with you."

There were elements of poor-little-rich-boy in what he was saying, but it did make sense. I couldn't imagine what the idea of billions did to some people. It scared the shit out of me. It made me cautious, made me not want to take advantage. Something told me Michael had been treated with reverence and envy, certainly jealously, but since he'd amassed his fortune he might not have been treated with care. He wanted what we all did, a partner who liked him for him and I think I was there.

I shook my head and glanced out the window.

"To add to that, you killed it with the NBA rep."

"Mr. Sands?" I failed to hide my pleasant surprise.

"Oh yeah. He loved you. I might have to take you to all my dinner meetings."

"Hmm. So what do we do now?"

He shrugged then glanced over at me. "That's up to you, but I'll be up front and say I like you and I want to see you again."

"Me too. I'd like to be your sugar baby, but I have to tell you up front that I am still really conflicted about this. It's—it's still weird for me. Like do you really pay me? Are you paying taxes on this? When can I see you again?"

"Yes, no, and you, Kayla, are welcome wherever I am."

"Jesus," I said with a snort. "Keep talking like that and you'll have a wife instead of a sugar baby."

"Give me time to buy a ring." I would've thought he was serious if he hadn't said it so casually. And if we'd known each other for more than two hours. And if I hadn't just agreed to let him be my literal sugar daddy.

"Ha. Funny. But really."

"I like having you around, if you wouldn't be bored out of your fucking mind I'd tell you to come to the office with me."

"Yeah, that might be a little dull. And I—"

"What?"

"I should still look for jobs."

He didn't respond.

"It's not that I'm not enjoying myself and I do appreciate the help. I just—"

He took my hand again. "Kayla. I know that this situation pretty much equates to you being a kept woman, but I get it. I could have retired twenty years ago, but I like to work. I like being productive. And so do you."

That was exactly it. I did appreciate that Michael was offering his financial support, but I wouldn't feel right just throwing in the towel and sitting on my ass. "Yeah. I have to do something."

"Then do something and tell me if you want my help. I can't hire you, but I can make some calls, see if anyone needs someone who's good at resourcing humans."

The minute he said the words, my heart pounded.

"You don't want to go back to HR, even in the meantime," he said.

"No. I loved my coworkers. I left some really good friends behind, but I hated that job. It was soul sucking."

"How about this? It's summer. Look for jobs. Look for stuff that interests you. You're bright, you seem like a fast learner, and I am not above making calls. If you find something you like, go for it."

"If I don't?"

"Take the summer and then, in the fall, go back to school or enroll in a graphic design course. I'll cover it."

That made the ache in my chest go away, but it was replaced by a twinge of something else.

"You don't want me to pay for it."

"No," I whined. What was wrong with me?

"I'd be annoyed if we weren't so alike. I understand not wanting a handout, but consider it this way, there is nothing wrong with accepting help. You won't have loan debt, you won't have to work two jobs to cover your expenses. And life is still life. Even if I pay for things I'm sure something else will come along to bite you in the ass in no time."

He was teasing me, but he had a point. There was nothing admirable about forcing myself to suffer and it wasn't like my work ethic would take a dive. I was too anal for that. I didn't have to turn into a lazy asshole, living off Michael until he got tired of me. I could use this time to make the positive moves I needed to make for myself.

"You're right, I'll looking into some programs for the fall. This is me time."

"Damn straight it is." Michael pulled to slow stop right in front of my building. Then he reached into his back pocket and pulled out a serious fold of cash.

"Was I that good?" I joked. Kinda.

"Not for the sex, that was priceless."

"Oh wow. That was awful."

"I know. It's for groceries and whatever else you and your roommate need. I'll have Ruben order you a debit card that's linked to one of my personal accounts. That should come in the next few days, but cash is always handy."

I took the bills, eyeing them a moment before I put them in my new purse. It was okay. I'd agreed to this. "Thank you."

"So would you be interested in seeing me again between now and the start of the semester?"

"Of course," I laughed. "Shut up. You're the

one with the crazy schedule."

"How about we have a little get together at my house this weekend? Invite some of your friends and we'll grill out by the pool." I'd missed the pool, but of course he had a pool.

"That doesn't qualify as partying on your dime?"

"It does, but I'm extending the invitation this time."

I did the quick mental math. "Is five people okay? That includes one guy."

"Five friends is fine." That damn mustache didn't cover up that smirk for shit.

"I mean I can put out a flyer on Facebook—"

"Five is perfect. Get them all here and I'll send a car. Day drinking in the sun doesn't make for safe driving conditions."

"Right. Good thinking. Well..." I held out my hand for a formal shake. "Thank you for taking this meeting with me, Mr. Bradbury. I think our companies can do business together."

He looked down at my hand. "You sure you want to leave it this way?"

I shook my head.

"Didn't think so," he said, and then he kissed me. And it was a good kiss, slow and soft, like we were breathing each other in, and just when I thought he would stop he'd come back for another nibble, another taste with his tongue.

"What if I don't want to wait until Saturday?" I asked.

"Then text me and I'm yours." And you know,

even though he was probably the busiest man in the world, I knew he was serious.

"I just—how?!" Adler was pacing in front of the couch and I was sitting there trying not to laugh, though I was pretty shocked myself. I expected Adler to still be asleep when I got home, but she was lying in front of the TV, wide awake, with a bowl of eggs, waiting for me to walk in the door. Not because she was worried about me of course, but because she wanted to grill me for details.

"You didn't even want to sign up with Arrangements and somehow you land the most eligible bachelor on the planet, with sugar baby benefits. Oh, he paid our rent by the way. The leasing office called me down to verify everything was cool."

"Already? He just left!"

"He paid it while you were in New York. He paid up the rest of our lease."

"What?"

"Yeah, through next March. How good are you at sucking dick?"

"Hey!"

She stopped pacing. "You did suck his dick, didn't you?" Then she practically slid onto my lap on the couch and I had to move over just to see her face without it blurring. "Oh please tell me you sucked his dick. Tell me all about his dick. Was it a nice dick?"

"Yes, his dick was very polite."

"Please, I'm begging you. Give me something."

"Okay, well he's sweet. He's honest and straightforward, which I like. He's kind."

"Yeah, yeah he's a very rich Boy Scout. Get to the good parts."

"He's a good kisser. He's really good at eating pussy. And he dicked me down real good last night."

"Oh my god, yes," she moaned.

"And this morning."

"Kayla!"

"What?!"

"I can't believe you snagged a guy that gorgeous and that rich. On the first try!"

"Thanks?"

"Sorry, I didn't mean it like that. I'd be shocked if anyone we knew had that kind of luck. So you're okay with the sex part of the arrangement I guess?"

"We had sex before we decided on *our* arrangement. But he didn't rush me into it and we'd kissed a bunch already and that made me want more."

"What do you think would have happened if you said no flat out?"

"Ah, nothing. He's not a rapist."

"No I know, but I mean like in terms of what he wants for his sugaring?"

I shrugged. "Guess we won't find out cause I already did it and I'm gonna do it again. After I talk to him about the rent."

"No, no. Don't. Let the rent thing slide. It's cool. It's fine. Be cool. 'Kay?"

I rolled my eyes. He had a little explaining to

do.

"You've made plans to hang out again, right? Or at least fuck again?"

"Hang out for sure. And the fucking. Pool party at his house on Saturday. You're invited. And between now and then...he said he's only a text away."

"Text him now and tell him to come back over so I can look at him."

"No," I said, laughing off her ridiculous suggestion, but I'd be lying if I said I didn't feel something close to jealousy. I felt possessive. That was it. I hadn't told Adler how I was really feeling about Michael, how I already missed him and how even though Saturday was only a few days away I wanted to see him that night. We definitely had an arrangement that didn't exactly make us boyfriend and girlfriend, but that didn't make him communal. "He has actual work to do. I'm not bothering him."

"Fine. Be greedy." Adler said, but she wasn't done interrogating me. She asked me about every second of our trip and gave my new handbag a thorough inspection. I'd done good for my first outing, she said.

By the time she'd finished her cross-examination, my first wind had worn off. I wanted to get some things done around the apartment and start a proper job search, but a late morning nap was calling my name. Adler's too. She'd barely slept while I was gone. I changed into my normal pajamas and, as I climbed into my small, normal bed with its below average thread count sheets, I texted my baby sister,

Kiara.

I have a new boyfriend and he's cuuuuuuute, followed by like eight smiley face emojis, and then I silenced my notifications.

When I didn't respond to her rapid-fire plea for details, she'd run to my other sister, Kaleigh, for information, but she'd do it right in front of my mom. That was their M.O. and how my mom usually kept tabs on me. They'd plant the seed of Michael's existence in my mom's head without me having to make an official declaration on his new place in my life. She'd bring him up the next time we talked.

Before I hunkered down for good this time though, I sent one more text. To Michael.

You covered the rest of our lease?!

He texted back about thirty seconds later.

I have no idea what you're talking about. Probably an anonymous donation.

And what if I'd said I didn't want to be your sugar baby?

You'd have to ask that anonymous donor.

Mhm. I still don't know why you picked me. There were a lot of cute girls at that sugar party.

Response time: about one minute. My picture

from my Arrangements profile popped up.

Because you're this beautiful all the time, even when you're nervous or sleeping in my lap with your mouth hanging open.
And the moment we met, I knew this beauty came from the inside.
Plus. That ass.

My laughter spurted out of me when I read that last bit, but my heart? It tripped over itself. He couldn't say things like that, things so sweet and observant. Those were the kinds of things that would make me fall in love.

He texted me again.

You want to see me tonight?

I thought about it for a moment, how it was probably a good idea to give us both some space. Give us both some time to process, to miss each other, but I already missed him. My hand was already typing before my brain caught up. He text me back right away. He'd be over to get me at eight.

Later in the afternoon, after some back and forth about the logistics of picking me up and driving back out to Malibu, only to drive me back to Miracle Mile in the morning, and after Michael casually explained that he was cool seeing me wherever and for however long because he had a full bathroom in his office complete with a shower and, of course, Ruben always made sure he had an extra set of clothes, I insisted we stay at my apartment that night. I didn't have a butler-cook and I didn't have a view, but we did have guest parking and a pizza place that delivered in twenty minutes right up the street. And then I remembered Adler would be there.

I decided to tell her last minute that Michael was coming over. I'd put my room back in order and showered. Kinda tried to make it look like I was getting ready for a quiet night in. Eight came and about five minutes after it went, Michael texted and said he was going to be late. Work stuff, but he was still coming. Work stuff was fine with me, but I was anxious as hell waiting for the right second to tell Adler that he was going to be in our apartment. I knew exactly how she was around really hot guys. And I'd seen her in action around really hot, rich, older guys. My plan was to get Michael in the door, quick introduction, then lock him in my bedroom with me until the morning. Behind my bedroom door there would be sex and enough cute conversation to make you puke.

My plan went completely to shit. Work stuff had Michael by the nuts until 11:30. I sat on the couch next to Adler through two full hours of *The Bachelorette* and three reruns of *Friends*. When he texted saying he was on the way, I just told her.

"Michael's coming over," I said as I tossed my phone onto the coffee table.

"Don't sound so excited."

"Eh."

"Well I'm excited. BRB." I ignored Adler as she left the room. When she came back something looked different, like she'd brushed her hair. When she sat down next to me I caught a whiff of something minty.

"Did you just brush your teeth?"

She tossed her hair and smiled at me. "No."

When Michael finally got to our place I went down to let him in. He knew I was cranky and tired as soon as he saw me.

He cupped my cheeks in his hands and kissed my lips. "I'm sorry."

"I might be too tired for sex."

An eyebrow popped up, and then he kissed me again. He had nice eyebrows. "That's understandable. It is late. Let's go upstairs and get you into bed."

When we got upstairs I let Adler get whatever she had to say out of her system. She hopped off the couch and held out her hand. I stood there as she introduced herself. Michael was perfectly polite, accepting Adler's thanks for the rent money and her praise for starting Arrangements. He was charming and sweet and they could wrap it up any fucking day now cause I was tired and more than ready to be spooned or banged to sleep.

When Adler asked him if he wanted to watch a movie and have some leftover pizza I may have groaned and leaned against the counter.

Michael laughed this little half-laugh, half-cough, making it clear we were on the same page. He wrapped his arms around my waist and pulled me upright. "I think I need to put my baby to bed."

"Aww Kay. He called you his baby."

"I know." It was sweet, but I was still cranky and annoyed.

"We'll see you in the morning, Adler. It was nice to meet you."

I grumbled my goodnight as he shuffled me in the general direction of my bedroom. I led him the rest of the way. The moment the door was closed he started to strip. I got into my bed and watched. He stopped at his boxers.

"Sorry I was so rude."

"Nah. Cranky Kayla is kinda cute."

"Just kinda? Oh fuck!"

Michael froze.

"I don't have any condoms. Let me ask Ads if—."

He reached down for his jeans and pulled out three condoms. Then stood up and put his hands behind his head. The whole motion made his hips jut out. He was definitely getting hard. "Thought you were too tired for sex."

I snuggled deeper under the covers. "Get in bed with me and we'll see what happens."

Chapter Five

Michael tossed the condoms on my nightstand then joined me under the sheets. He was completely hard now. He pulled me closer, spooning me with his dick pressed against my ass. I was already pretty hot and bothered just from seeing him step out of his car, but I wanted to beg him to use one of those condoms when he kissed the shell of my ear.

"How was your day, dear?" he said quietly.

I waited to answer because his hand was sliding over my stomach and getting seriously close to the band on my pajama pants. And then his hand was in my underwear. I tried not to move. Still, I couldn't help but press back against him as his fingers found my wet slit. The feeling—the perfectly deliberate search for my clit, teasing it just a little before pushing his way farther between my thighs—I wanted it all night.

"Tell me about your day," he said. He wanted to hear me talk while I was trying not come in the first five minutes of our night.

A deep breath rushed out of my lungs as I managed to squeak out an answer. "It was okay. I thought about you a lot."

"I thought about you."

"You did?"

"It's nice to have someone to think about."

"You can't say stuff like that when you're touching me like this."

"Why?"

"Because it's not fair. Oh fuck." He'd pulled my pajama bottoms down with his other hand, and his dick... I could feel the smooth hardness of it, every inch rubbing against my ass. I was going to come or ask him to put a baby in me. I didn't know which would happen first.

"I'm just telling you how it is. I like thinking about you."

"I like thinking about you too. Will you—?"

His hands and my hips stopped moving.

"Will I what?"

He moved with me, giving me space to roll over and face him. He was so gorgeous. That long dark hair spilled all over my white pillowcases, and his face. I could see the lines around his eyes and the bags underneath them. But that glint, that shine and passion that still made it hard for me to believe the truth in our age difference, was there in that perfect shade of blue. I wanted to tell him what I needed to happen next. He was just so gentle and sweet and almost playful, I didn't know how he would take it.

He moved a bit of my hair off my cheek. "What is it?"

"You're...great. I love how you treat me. All of this, the kisses and the way you touch me—I mean, holy fuck you're a good kisser."

"You are too."

"Thank you. I was just hoping we could—last time was hot. Like way hot. I was just wondering if you could fuck me like really hard."

He hid his surprise really well, but I was already starting to notice his little quirks. That eyebrow wanted to launch itself into space, but he caught it.

"It's you," I continued, while I reached down and stroked his dick between us, rubbing the precum on my stomach. His eyes closed for a few seconds as I kept up the rhythm. "You're just so sexy. And so sweet. It makes me wish you were not so sweet."

That opened his eyes. "I'm always going to be good to you, Kayla."

"I know and that makes me want you to hang me upside down off the side of the bed and fuck me like a pogo stick. I can handle it a little rough."

"That was very specific. So you like it a little freaky."

"I'd like it that way with you, and the sweet stuff too. Also I'm okay with butt stuff, just go slow."

"Butt stuff. Go it. We can do rough. You have to let me know your limits though."

"I will. What's it called? A safe word. Let's go with 'hold on', 'wait' and 'stop'."

That little smile was going to kill me. "Those work just fine,"

"Okay so where were we? You had your dick on my ass—"

"I want something else now."

"Oh?"

"Grab me one of those."

The second I rolled over and reached for one of the condoms, Michael's hand came down on my ass. Hard. I yelped, but didn't move out of his reach when he did it again. The third time he smacked my cheeks and then gave one a firm squeeze. I was worried that it might be too much ass for him, but he was handling it just fine.

"Come here." An arm came around my waist and he pulled me on top of him, making the breath rush out of my lungs. He was fucking strong. We were both upright, Michael with his back against my headboard and me on top, facing him, straddling his lap. "Put the condom on," he said. And after I did, then he pulled me closer, his hands gripping my hips. I was ready to sit right on top of his erection, but he wouldn't let me. He grabbed both my breasts instead, one in each hand and then he went right for my nipples.

I always liked having my nipples touched and played with. They are so sensitive, kissing them or sucking them was a surefire way to turn me on. A pregame if you will, to get the crowd excited. I was already excited, more than wet. He licked and sucked at me, one breast then the other, back and forth, while my hips took control and forced my clit up and down the length of his shaft. I wanted to come, needed to come, but I wanted him inside me so bad.

I begged.

"Michael. Please."

He just shook his head. And then he pushed my breasts together and started licking both nipples at once. I looked down at him, hair tousled, tongue out and I came so hard, my body shivering as I tried to pull away for that moment my body needed to process the pleasure.

That was when he pulled me up and sat me down on his hard cock with what I think was only a fraction of his real strength. That just made the orgasm worse or better. I don't know. I think I blacked out.

Michael fucked me, that strong hand of his going to the back of my head while he kissed me and his other hand slapping my ass, spanking me in perfect rhythm with thrusts. My butt was on fire, but it felt so good. I came again, shaking against this perfect man inside me.

He didn't stop.

I was still on top, but I wasn't riding him. I was just holding on for dear life, praying we didn't break the bed or my pelvis.

"Is this good?" he panted against my neck.

"Yeah. Yes. Oh my god. Yes."

"I'd flip you over, but I love looking at your face when you come."

"We'll do that. Soon. We have to. We owe it to each other. We've earned it. But don't stop."

He didn't stop.

His hands gripped my hips and he kept fucking me and fucking me until I think I just became one long, living, breathing orgasm. Until he eventually came. I fell off of him, rolling onto my stomach cupping myself between my legs. I'd never walk again. Michael did something, probably got rid of the condom, I don't know. I had like two of my senses left and neither of them was filling in my brain's request for information. And then he was kissing me again, soft wet kisses down the length of my back. I was practically in a coma, but feeling his lips on my skin somehow woke my clit up. She was ready for more. My vagina was not.

I rolled onto my side and Michael joined me, spooning my back as he pulled the sheet over as both. I wrapped my arm around his, holding him closer, letting the feel of weird stuff like the hair on his arm and the ridges of his knuckles ground me in reality.

His lips brushed my ear again. "How did I do?" he asked.

"You did great. That was some A-plus fucking, Mr. Bradbury."

"Next time I'll go for extra credit."

"You're lucky I like corny cause that was horrible." His chest shook a little, a rare bit of genuine laughter, and then he kissed my neck. I wondered if he had any idea how badly I wanted to keep him.

"Oh my god. You two were so fucking loud." That was the first thing Adler said to me the next morning when I came out of my room. Michael was long gone. I hated sleeping in, but I woke up in the middle of the night with his head between my legs and I wanted to return the favor and then things got a little out of control. After, I was knocked out, but I remembered him kissing my face a few times as he said goodbye.

When I finally did wake up, a little after ten,

there were a few sweet Michael texts on my phone, telling me how much he'd enjoyed last night and how he was available if I needed him. My brain was still an oversexed mess so I decided to get breakfast squared away before I answered. Didn't want to say something stupid or way over the top, like *I love you, marry me now.*

When I looked up from my phone, Adler was staring at me over her bowl of cereal.

"I'm sorry. We got a little carried away."

"Twice. Have you always been that loud of a fucker?"

"I don't know," I laughed. "Maybe."

"Well color me jealous. Whatever the hell you two were doing sounded pretty hot. I almost called up Shaner for a quick bang-and-dash just to take the edge off."

"Oh god, please do not call Shaner. Ever. I don't care how horny you are. I'll go down on you before I tell you Shaner's a safe idea." Adler's loser ex was usually on the 'do not *mention*' list so we must have put on some show. "What do you have going on today?" I asked.

She made a face like it was ridiculous question then shrugged. "Nothing?"

"I'm gonna look for some more jobs, then hit Ralph's. Michael gave us grocery money."

"I'm sorry, I thought I just heard you say you were going to look for jobs."

"Yeah. Why, what's wrong with that?"

"Kay, you hit the fucking jackpot. Enjoy it."

I didn't feel comfortable telling Adler that

Michael had basically said the same thing mostly because I didn't want her to encourage us to be lazy as a roommate unit. Technically she still had to find a Sugar Daddy of her own or a job. Michael had covered a lot of both our needs, but what if we ended our arrangement? It wasn't something I wanted to think about, but I had to.

"I don't think it's a good idea for either of us to depend on him like that," I said, trying to keep my tone light.

"Why? He totally likes you."

"Right, but what if something happens and we call it quits? We should both be prepared for that."

"God, that's bleak. But I guess you're right. I'll keep looking too."

I felt bad for pooing on her party, but facts was facts. "How about this? I need a new bathing suit—"

"Yes?" Adler stood up.

"And the rent is covered. And Michael did give me way more than enough for groceries and the light bill, so I have a tiny bit of wiggle room in my savings—"

"Yes?" She walked around the table and took me by the shoulders.

"You wanna go shopping?"

"Yes! Oh god, yes!" She shook me then ran off to her room shrieking something unintelligible.

My gut told me to tell Michael. Technically I was spending my money, but his money was making it possible for me to spend my money. I was overthinking it, I knew but still. I wanted to feel one hundred percent right about it. I texted him a sweet good morning and then told him that I was going to buy Adler and I new bathing suits for his pool party, if that was okay with him.

His response time: twenty seconds. He must have had a free moment.

What's your favorite color?

Um random, but it's blue. I started to text and then I knew what he was getting at so I added, *I look good in blue too.*

Send lewd pictures from the dressing room.

LOL Ewww no

I tried.

Then my phone rang. It was my mom.

Telling my mom as much as I could about the current state of my life without confessing that things were taken care of and I didn't have to stress about finding a new job thanks to my literal sugar daddy took a little finessing.

I gave up his name, but not his last name. I mentioned he was older just not how much older. I told her that Michael worked in the tech field and yes like the Internet and that seemed to end that line of questioning.

She didn't know how fucked my financial situation was before I met Michael so I didn't bring that up of course. When she asked about my job search I tried to sound optimistic.

When the girls started screaming in the background asking for Michael's full name I told her I had to go. She wasn't too, too concerned about any guy a week into a relationship, so she didn't care much more about his particulars, but she would if things got serious. I tried not to think of the pressure that getting serious carried, grabbed my roommate and my purse and headed out the door.

I didn't see Michael again before we arrived at his house in a chauffeur driven Suburban. He was super busy over the next two days and I passed on an opportunity to do some business related clubbing with him on Friday. I wanted to see him, but I wanted him to myself. I was a little worried that I was violating the terms of our arrangement, but he texted me later telling me the night had gone to shit, a deal had fallen through and he was glad I wasn't there to witness him cuss someone out. I couldn't imagine him getting really angry, but I was glad I'd missed the drama.

The backseat of the Suburban was almost

bouncing when we pulled up to Michael's house. It wasn't me, but my friends were pretty amped to be there. Daniella and Gordo, my best friends from my former HR department, Sienna and Adler, were like little kids pulling up to the pearly gates of Disneyland the closer we got to the closed off and clearly exclusive part of Malibu. I just wanted to see Michael.

He walked out his front door just as we pulled up the driveway. As soon as I saw him I knew I was spending the night. He was barefoot, wearing nothing but a pair of blue and orange board shorts. His hair was up in this messy yet sexy-as-hell bun. It was definitely on.

"That's him," Adler said with a little bit of pride. I laughed it off when I saw the look on Daniella's face.

"Um, can I borrow your daddy?" she teased.

"Can we all borrow your daddy?" Gordo added. "He is fine as fuck."

I shook my head and just laughed. I knew PJ could hear us.

I hopped out of the car and managed not to sprint over and jump on Michael. Instead I walked into his arms and took a short kiss. My friends were there, crossing the perfectly poured concrete, but for that few seconds all his attention was on me. He took my cheeks in his hands and kissed me again.

"Hi," was all he said. I needed to record his voice for bedtime. Or wank sessions.

"Hi."

Another moment, just me and him. And then we both shook it off and turned to my friends. They behaved themselves as I did introductions, even though I could tell Adler was dying to give him shit about our excessively loud fucking.

"Why don't you guys come on in? I'll give you the tour."

There was a round of "okay, sure"s, but I didn't miss Sienna saying "I wouldn't mind you giving me of a bit of *your* tour" and Adler's hysterical giggle after Michael took my hand and led the way inside.

First stop on the tour was the kitchen. And Holger.

"Look at this motley crew," he said as we walked in. I think we were all a little too afraid to respond, but I managed a polite hello. Holger was something close to six and a half feet tall and three feet wide. He had a white mohawk and handlebar mustache, and a German accent. He was prepping a bunch of burgers and steaks while wearing two parts of a three-piece suit with the sleeves on his pinstripe shirt rolled up. He had tattoos all over his hands. "Is this the lady?" he asked, nodding in my direction.

Michael pulled me forward and kissed me on my temple. "This is Kayla." He introduced my friends as well, but Holger seemed more focused on me.

"He didn't sell your beauty. We should take his business degrees away."

"That is an outrage. Just show me where they are and I'll toss them right in the shredder," I said, bumping Michael with my hip.

"I like her. She stays. I have enough food for a whole army. I hope you're all prepared to be stuffed," he said to the group.

"Bad choice of words, man," Michael said. "They're already scared of you. We'll be back."

Michael took us around his ridiculously large house with its weight room and screening room and its amazing views of the mountains and the ocean, then brought us back to the kitchen, where Holger had apparently finished preparing his bounty.

"Everybody grab a tray and out to the pool we go." My friends and I were still a little stunned by his overall presence, but he had the command of a calm and gentle third grade teacher, so we all grabbed what we could carry and fell in line behind him. Well I tried, but Michael lightly touched my arm and asked me to hang back.

"What's up?" I asked when we were alone.

"Just wanted to talk for a minute."

He led me to the white stools that lined the massive kitchen island. I sat. He stood.

"Uh oh, good talk or bad talk?"

"I hope it's a good talk."

I closed my eyes and took a deep breath then gave my body a good shake. "Okay, go."

"I wanted to check in with you. See how you're feeling about us."

"I feel good about us and a little nervous about us."

"What makes you nervous?" When he asked I could tell he almost reached up and touched my face, but he kept his hands to himself, which I was grateful for. His touch made me weak. And horny.

"I know we have an arrangement—" Air

quotes were necessary. "But I think when I told you that there had to be feelings there, I wasn't sure that would or could be true with you, but clearly..."

"I like being with you too. We don't have to have some big-where-is-this-going conversation. Just wanted a general read on the situation."

"I agree. We enjoy being together so let's just roll with that and see where it goes."

"That's sounds like a perfect plan. Would you like to stay with me tonight?"

"Yes," I said with a firm nod. Michael smiled at that.

"Good, glad that's all settled."

"It's rude to have sex while there's guests in the house, right?"

"I think it's frowned upon, but don't worry." He came closer and slipped his hand around the side of my neck as he kissed me. I touched him too, resting my fingers along the dusting of hair that ran down his stomach.

"We have plenty of time," he said when we finally took a breather. He was right, but the last thing I wanted to do was go outside to socialize. I wanted my Michael time.

Still we headed toward the pool.

Chapter Six

I had to say the view and the pool, hell, the whole scene, kind of made up for our lack of privacy. There were hidden speakers around the yard, playing perfect pool-side party music. Michael took over the grill for Holger, who disappeared back inside to tear phone books in half or something. I don't know.

My friends had made themselves comfortable on various lounge chairs. Adler stripped off her shorts and tank top and dove right into the pool. I was eyeing the massive cabana complete with a fire pit that looked like the perfect place for Michael to fuck my brains out, but I hung by the grill and grabbed both of us a beer from a short barrel full of ice I imagined Holger had put out before we arrived.

Michael took a sip of his drink then reached out for me. He kissed me on the temple when I stepped closer. I was starting to love that little gesture. It was so damn sweet.

"You can go sit with your friends if you want," he said, nuzzling the scruff of his beard against my face. It was already starting to lose some of its crispness from his visit to the barbershop. I moved closer, pressing myself against his side.

"I know, but I want to be with you. What exactly went awry last night?"

Michael went on to explain how he'd been

asked to invest in a film and how he and Ruben met with the writer/producer who was trying to secure the funding. The guy was a total dick, apparently, and kept hitting on Ruben while claiming he was straight and using slurs. The strange things insecure people do. So Michael had a few choice words for the guy, then split. He took Ruben with him of course.

"Do you still want to invest in a film or was it something about this guy in particular?"

"It was a favor for a friend, but I have thought about putting some money behind a worthy project."

"I'm sure there are plenty of programs that work with indie filmmakers, filmmakers of color, gay and lesbian film makers and stuff that would love your money. Maybe you can look into something like that, instead of doing favors for douches," I said, looking up at him with a wide smile.

"That's a good idea."

"I'm full of them."

I wanted to ask Michael what the upcoming week looked like for him but more guests arrived. Interesting guests.

I turned around as I heard someone call his name. And that somebody was Duke Stone, probably the most famous pop star of the moment, and he wasn't alone. I recognized a few of the guys with him as his backup singers and band mates. They had a couple girls with them, who all smiled and said hello to Michael and me. But I wasn't too focused on them.

I'd had a fangirl crush on Duke since his amazing Super Bowl halftime show a few years before and I'd been trying to get tickets to one of his shows forever. And now Michael was introducing us. I almost swallowed my tongue.

"You didn't tell me you had a new boo-thang," Duke joked.

Michael laughed. "I didn't want you to steal her away from me before I locked it down." I could feel my cheeks burning up, part embarrassment, part giddiness. Duke Stone was standing in front of me and Michael was talking about me to him.

Duke and his crew introduced themselves to my friends and settled in around the pool.

"We met at a Knicks game a while ago and we've been friends ever since," Michael said when they were out of earshot.

All I could come up with was "That's so cool."

Soon the first round of burgers and steaks were coming off the grill and we all started to settle into the scene. A few more people showed up, mega movie stars Chris Ryan and Chris Mitchell, the current kings of summer blockbusters, with I think at least one girlfriend and maybe her friend, but that was it. I think Michael was going for casual fun in the sun and not poolside rager.

Eventually Holger came back out to act as host, manning the grill and collecting empties. One of the Chris girls and I tried to help with the clean-up, but we were immediately shooed away. I thought about joining the chaos in the pool, but decided against it when Michael led me over to the cabana. We lay down on the white cushions and I settled against him. We didn't talk, just watched the party unfold. I liked that we could be quiet together just as much as we could talk about anything.

Daniella joined us and started giving me the latest office gossip. I couldn't believe how much I missed her and Gordo. When I started, Gordo was the only brown person in our department. We bonded and pulled Daniella into our circle of necessity when she was hired three months after me. We always joked that we made up three sides of the perfect rainbow triangle; me being black and bisexual, Gordo being Mexican and gay, and Daniella being Afro-Cuban and transgender. We'd become so close, not being able to see them every day was almost as hard as losing my benefits and a steady paycheck.

"Oh and Cruiser got fired," Daniella said. Her office crush was one of the main reasons she showed up every morning. "But that had nothing to do with the merger."

Just as I was about to ask about Fredrick, our supervisor and the office drunk, the song blasting through the speakers changed to one of Duke's most popular hits. You'd think it would be cheesy for him and his boys to hop out of the pool and start doing the full stage routine to "Stunner", complete with so much air guitar and air trumpet, but it was almost better than going to an actual show. They were so loose and sun-toasted, and a little drunk, you could see how much fun they were having acting up.

And then Duke came over and grabbed Daniella. Her light brown cheeks flashed red, but that didn't stop her from following his lead as he twirled her around then pulled her down on his lap.

When the song finished he kissed her on the

cheek, then released her back into the shelter of the cabana. She immediately curled up in a giggling ball against my knees. I almost died laughing.

"Are you okay?" I asked.

"I can't breathe. Oh my god, I cannot fucking breathe." When she looked up her face was comically red. "Can you be outrageously aroused and stunned speechless at once?"

"Don't believe those things are mutually exclusive," Michael said with his own chuckle.

"Is it like this at your house all the time?" Daniella asked.

"No. Unfortunately."

"Probably." Michael and I said at the same time.

"Well I also have massive crushes on a few other famous people, if you want to invite them over."

"Make me a list and I'll get it to my people," Michael teased.

"I love him, Kayla. Marry him."

"Sounds good. I'm on it."

Daniella stood up and bounced in a circle. "Bye!" She squealed then dove back into the pool.

"My friends like you."

"They like this." Michael's tone was light, but he wasn't exactly lying. My friends didn't know him. And I...

I sat up and turned to face him. "I like you."

He reached up and touched my breast, brushing my nipple through my clothes. "You said something about picking up a new bathing suit."

I glanced down to where his fingers were now tugging at the bottom of my shirt. I was still in my shorts too.

"Do you want to see it?"

"Yes. I would like that."

I shifted off the cushions and started pulling off my clothes. It had taken me a little while to find the right suit, but one of my favorite stores that actually had a reliable plus-size section came through. I revealed the high-waisted bikini with its fringy top that bled from orange at the straps to purple on the bottom. I turned around so Michael could see how big and juicy my butt looked in it, but the applause came from the pool.

"Sexy mama!" Adler yelled.

"Looking good, girl!" came from one of Duke's boys. I did a little curtsy then turned back to Michael. "What do you think?"

"Come over here."

I crawled back over to him, bracing myself over his perfect chest. Michael slid his hand down my side and grabbed my ass. I pushed back a little, wiggling my butt in his grasp. "You still have company, you know."

"I can kick them out."

"That would be rude. Like you said, we have time." I leaned a little closer and whispered in his ear. "Will you finger me later?"

"I'll do it right now," he replied, his tone deathly serious.

"I'll be in the pool." There was nothing I wanted more than to drag Michael into the house and spend the rest of the day with various parts of him inside various parts of me, but I knew if we left our friends for a little something-something I'd try to turn our little quickie into an all-day-er. I walked over to the pool steps and slipped in next to Adler and Gordo. I thought Michael would join us, but as he stood up Holger came out of the house and handed Michael the phone. Always working.

We pool-partied into the night. More singing from Duke, drunken shallow-end games of chicken, plenty of food and maybe a few too many beers for me, though I hid it well. I was loose for sure, and becoming that drunk kind of aroused that happens when you're tipsy and in the company of the person you've kind of been waiting all day to screw. Michael had to take a few calls throughout the afternoon and evening. The Internet never sleeps after all, but he always came back to me with a kiss or a gentle touch.

The mood started to change close to ten. I was toasting marshmallows with Daniella and Michael around the fire pit. Duke came over to join us. Well, to join Daniella. He'd been orbiting her all day, flirting a little then walking away, but he always seemed to come back. Michael and I watched them for a bit, but I looked away when Duke started whispering in her ear. It was one of those whispers that was either the precursor to a kiss or getting up and finding a private corner where they could get to know each other better. That made me think I'd waited long enough for my own bit of private time, but when I turned to do some whispering of my own, I caught a glimpse of Adler in the hot tub on the lap of one of the Chrises. She was making out with one the girls that had shown up with Duke and his friends.

I'd reached my limit, but I didn't even have to say anything. Eye contact with Michael was all it took to make him grab my hand and usher me inside. We went straight to his bedroom. I flopped on the bed and started peeling off my shirt, which I'd put back on after the sun set. My bikini followed. Michael watched. I could see his erection growing.

"How would you like it tonight?" Michael asked as he unzipped the hoodie he'd thrown on.

I slipped my hand between my legs, the alcohol in my system making me feel a little bolder than usual. "Why don't you decide."

We stared at each other as he undid the drawstring on his board shorts and let them fall to the floor. Definitely hard now. He held my gaze as he reached for a condom and tossed it on the nightstand. Held my gaze still as he dug up something to tie his hair back.

I slid a finger inside my pussy to tease us both a little more. I think he liked it. "Hair's going up. Are you about to put in some work?"

"If by work you mean banging you to sleep, then yeah."

"And then what?" I don't even know why I said it, but something, some shadow, something he was trying to hide crossed over Michael's face. I knew that flinch, that little tick. It wasn't anything bad, but something intense. Something he wasn't ready to share. I knew that feeling. I'm sure I'd hidden the same look on my own face plenty of times. It was almost the kind of thing that could ruin the mood. Almost.

Michael reached down and wrapped his arms around my thighs. I tried not to scream, but a high-pitched squeak did slip out. He yanked me to the edge of the bed, then sunk to his knees right in front of me.

"You said you wanted my fingers," he said as he pushed two fingers inside of me and all the air out of my lungs. I swallowed and managed something close to a frantic nod. "Did you want any other part of me? Or will the fingers be enough?"

I shook my head. It helped me shake away the stupid thing I was going to say. "I want some dick too. And your mouth."

"We can do that." I followed his gaze as he looked down and watched his fingers slide in and out of my pussy. I slid closer, eliminating the small space between us. I had to kiss him. And he almost let me. Our lips brushed together but he pulled away, just a little. Enough for me to see those gorgeous eyes. "At the right time, I'm going to ask you something important, but not right now. Okay?" he said, voice filled with promise and what I suspected might almost be a confession of love.

It was low. So, so low, hinting that he felt the same way about me as I did him when he was almost wrist deep in the one part of my body that loved to try and override my brain. But he was right. I wasn't ready. I knew what he was starting to mean to me. I knew the kind of time, the kind of relationship I wanted from him. The dedication and not just the words, but the follow-through. And maybe that's what scared me the most.

If working in HR taught me anything, it was how to read people, to see where they fit. Actually, the job made me see that I'd always been good at knowing who was right and wrong for who and what. I'd read the man between my legs, taken in every word, every signal and vibe. Michael Bradbury didn't play games. Michael Bradbury would follow through and deliver on every single thing I wanted because he was telling me right now that he wanted those things too.

He said what he meant and when there was silence he told on himself with every line in his face and every movement of his hands. So when he pulled me closer with a gentle grip on the back of my neck and finally kissed me, kissed me the way I wanted him to instead of withholding his affection until he got the answer out of me that he wanted, I knew then that I was in way too deep to try to tell myself that I didn't want this to go the distance. But I wasn't ready yet. This wasn't the right moment. I needed more time, but I wanted Michael Bradbury to myself.

I lightly tugged on his wrist and when his hand was free, I pulled him on top of me. But he stopped, just long enough to slip the condom on, because that's what I wanted him to do. Later, whenever he asked whatever he wanted to ask me, I was going to say yes.

Saturday rolled into Sunday and the party seemed to go with it. We lost a few people. The Chrises had to go and their girls went with them, along with most of Duke's crew, who I think disappeared in the night. The Chrises were headed in Sienna's direction and offered to drop her off. Gordo had a family thing that he was way late for by the time Holger roused us for brunch. PJ drove him back to his place. Michael and I managed to get out of the bed, hangover-free and, after we got dressed (Michael had more clothes brought to the house for me), joined Duke and Daniella, Adler and two of Duke's bandmates down in the screening room. Michael had every movie ever, but Adler wanted to watch *Inception*. That rolled into *The Dark Knight Rises*.

I slipped out to use the bathroom between movies and on the way back I ran into Holger in the hallway. "Everything up and up?" he asked. I looked up at him and tried not to stare. He was so confusing, mostly because of the accent and the mohawk.

"Yeah, thank you for breakfast and lunch and yesterday."

"Not a problem. This is for you." He handed me a sky-blue business card. There was no name on it, just a number in yellow print. "You need the slightest thing, you call me."

"Will you tell me where you bury the bodies?"

"No, never." His feigned shock made me

laugh. "A man's got to have his secrets. But I am as much yours as I am his."

"I'll make sure I hide this from my roommate. She might 911 you just to get us some more of your good cooking."

He shook his head. "I don't answer to roommates. Only the Mister and his lady."

"Wow, that's heavy." I let out a sigh. "Thanks. I'll save the number in my phone, then burn this so my roommate doesn't get her hands on it."

"Perfect. Ah and his fiftieth is coming up. Big party. Big. We'll see you there?"

"Ah yeah. If he asks me to come." Not that he wouldn't, but he hadn't mentioned it yet.

"You'll be the second guest of honor." I took his wink as my cue to get back to the screening room. I thanked him again, then set off on my way.

"Good?" Michael asked, as I curled up next to him.

I showed him Holger's card. "He keeps calling me your lady."

"He might keep calling you that forever. It took me six years to get him stop calling me Mikey."

"Oh god. That's awful."

"Hey, down in front! Shut up!" Duke yelled from three cushions behind. We were talking over the great plane kidnapping scene in the opening, which we'd all seen seven hundred times.

Michael reached for the remote and paused the movie. "You were saying?" he asked me.

I snorted, covering my face.

"Fuckers." That was Adler, but I don't think

she threw the piece of pastry that whizzed by our heads.

I grabbed the remote and hit play. "I will never call you Mikey."

"And I promise only to call you my lady behind your back."

"So it's your fault?"

Michael pulled me closer and kissed my face. "Uh-hm."

You know what will make you hate the geographical layout of Los Angeles County? Realizing just how far away your apartment is from your boyfriend's house, especially when you didn't bring your own car out to his house and your roommate is looking at you with puppy dog eyes when the driver shows up to take her home. Her. Not you. Michael had to go into the office and, after a week of dicking around, I did need to get back on top of my job search, but I just wanted a few more hours alone with him.

Just sitting there watching movies with him was perfect. There were a few texts from Ruben, but he didn't take any calls. But still, we had company. By dinner time our party had whittled down to Adler, Duke, Daniella, Michael and I. Duke got called to the studio after we had pizza delivered for dinner and Daniella admitted that she should probably get back. She actually had a job. Michael had PJ come around to pick her up. I debated going with them or staying, but when Adler asked me if I was coming, even though I resented the shit out her for even suggesting it, I remembered how out of the way our place was from his office.

I packed up my shit and did my best not to stamp my feet and cry while Adler and Daniella waited for me to get into the SUV. Michael's kissing didn't make it any better.

"Why do you live so far?" I said with a pout.

"You want me to buy your apartment building? I'll move over by you. Or maybe I'll set Adler up somewhere else and move in with you."

My heart jumped into my throat, but I managed not to choke on it. I swallowed and looked down at his bare feet on his smooth driveway. "Yes, please. Buy a building so I never have to go home. Sext me before you go to bed?"

"Anything you want. I'll sext you real good."

"'Kay." I stood up on my tiptoes and kissed him for an obnoxiously long time. The blaring of the horn was the only thing that pulled us apart. And Adler yelling over PJ's shoulder for me to come the fuck on. I kissed Michael one last time then jumped into the car. We hadn't even pulled out of the driveway and I was thinking about seeing him again.

"What are you all smiley about?" Adler teased Daniella, as we made our way toward the PCH.

"Duke and I swapped numbers. He wants to hang out."

"What the fuck?!" Adler said, flopping back on the seat cushions.

I looked up from my phone. "What?"

"What does a girl gotta do around here?"

"Stop asking what a girl's gotta do?" I said.

"Jesus. I was kidding. Sensitive much."

"I'm just saying. He likes her. You're making it sounds like she plotted her way into his contacts." It was too late for me to realize how annoyed I was with her, I think, or maybe I was just tired. I decided it would be best if I stopped talking and retreated into my email on my phone. It would be bad for all of us if I said what was really on my mind.

Adler reached over and patted Daniella's leg. "I didn't mean it like that."

"I know," Daniella replied. "She's just cranky. She misses her boo already. Don't blame you, Kay. He's pretty awesome."

"Yeah. He's pretty swell." My inbox rolled over and loaded my new messages. There was an email from Monica Lawrence. Social Manager with Arrangements. The subject said "Next Steps". I opened it, ignoring Daniella and Adler's chatter.

Good Morning Kayla! I spoke with Mr. Bradbury and am delighted to hear that you two have been spending time together. If you would like to continue seeing Mr. Bradbury we just ask that you set your profile to dormant on the Arrangements website. Currently your profile is still visible to all of the great men in our dating pool and we'd hate for some poor guy to think he still has a chance with you. You can access the dormant option through your profile settings. Please let me know if you have any questions.

Luck in love, Monica

There was also an email from Ruben. The subject said "Save the Date."

Hay Kay, Michael's fiftieth birthday is a month away. A formal invite to his surprise party should be in your mailbox tomorrow morning, but I wanted to give you the deets...

The rest of the email outlined the plans for the night, and what Ruben hoped would be my role in getting Michael to the venue, and firm instructions to use the account Michael had set up for me to get my hair and wardrobe in order. My new debit card should be in my mail along with the invitation. I emailed Ruben back, telling him I was on board, and asked him for the exact date of his birthday. Then I emailed Monica back, thanking her for the instructions. Then I logged into Arrangements and deleted my account.

Chapter Seven

"I'll be back on Monday morning," I told Adler as I tossed my overnight tote onto my shoulder. In the three weeks since our tense moment in the backseat of Michael's suburban things between us had gone back to normal. Friends get snippy with each other sometimes. It happens.

"Sienna and I are hitting the movies tonight and then I will be here. On this couch. Looking for jobs."

"Good." Michael was still helping us with groceries and stuff like gas, but I refused to use his money for recreational spending that didn't involve him.

Adler was still looking for a job. She'd had two promising interviews for assistant positions, but still hadn't heard anything back yet. I was pretty sure Sienna was comping her movie ticket.

I was still looking for a new job, but I had also jumpstarted my graphic design work. One of Michael's buddies had pointed me to some online do-at-your-pace design tutorials. I'd become obsessed with perfecting my typography skills. They'd come in handy for what I'd planned for the night.

I said bye to Adler, then headed outside to meet Michael. I told him point-blank that I wanted to spend his birthday night in, just the two of us. He didn't suspect the surprise party that was still on for the following weekend, but we always talked about spending more time together. His schedule didn't bother me. He worked hard and I'd be lying if I said his drive and his success weren't massive turn-ons, but absence and the heart and whatnot. I missed him when we were apart and I think he missed me. We were always texting and, when his schedule allowed, we were together, either at my place or his. We tried to keep it down when Adler was home. My phone was slowly starting to fill up with pictures of him or selfies of us together. It was all very couple-y.

Well, really, I was in love, but I hadn't told Michael yet. And I think he was at least falling in love with me too, but he had yet to say so. And he still hadn't asked me whatever he wanted to ask me.

I tried not to think about either of those things too much. I just enjoyed my time with him and tried to believe that this amazing guy and the amazing way he treated me was not too good to be true.

I pulled his hand into my lap and asked him about work as we made our way to Malibu. The NBA deal was closer to becoming a reality. The a certain team's owner needed to step away. He was a million years old and his estate didn't want to will the team to his family. The general feeling in the locker room matched that sentiment. The players wanted him to sell. There were a lot of politics involved and Michael had to walk a certain walk even if he decided not to make a serious bid for the team. The whole thing made me happy for him, but nervous at the same time.

"I can't conceptualize having enough money to buy a team," I said, as we hopped out of the car and walked through the front door. "I'm still psyched that I bought my own car and I couldn't keep my job long enough to pay it off. Capitalism, man. Never a dull moment."

Michael laughed. "That is definitely true. Holger said he was making dinner tonight. I hope you're in the mood for salmon."

"Actually I talked to Holger. There's been a change in the menu. This way please."

I grabbed Michael's hand and led him into the kitchen. Holger was waiting for us and everything was set up exactly the way I wanted it. Fifty cupcakes with gold and white frosting, spelling out the numbers five zero were in the middle of the counter, along with the birthday cards I'd spent two weeks designing on my computer. And there was a platter of Philly Cheesesteaks from Michael's favorite dive restaurant and a frosty bucket of cold beers.

"Happy Birthday to you..." I started to sing in hushed, slightly off key tones. Holger joined in and Michael graciously let us finish the song.

"I skipped the candles because I kept having these weird visions of your beard catching on fire."

"That's fair."

"But I made the cupcakes myself, and I made the cards, and I paid for dinner with my savings. This is a birthday brought to you by Kayla."

Holger held up his hands and took a step back. "I helped with presentation. That's it."

"Thank you both. I appreciate it."

We took a seat and dug into our dinner. I tried to get Holger to join us, but he insisted that Michael should spend his birthday evening alone with his lady. I rolled my eyes and didn't argue when he booked it for the pool house.

Michael picked up one of the cards and flicked it open again. He kept toying with them. "I'm impressed with these."

"The artwork or my clever poetry?" Both cards had vintage, 70's designs on the front. One had a sweet note inside, and the other had a dirty limerick pretty much telling Michael I was still happy to fuck him even though he was a half-century-old. I was proud of that one.

"Both. You're good. I think you should stick with this."

"Maybe I'll start a greeting card line. Naughty Notes by Kayla."

"Don't joke around. I'll get it up and running."

I leaned over and kissed him. "That's why I love you. You're so sweet to me."

"When you're ready, I want you to move in with me," he said quietly.

"Is that what you wanted to ask me this whole time?"

He looked down for a second and took my hand, but then he looked into my eyes. "I don't want what I'm feeling to rule what's happening between us. But I want you to know where I'm coming from."

"Best to make decisions with all the available information at hand?"

"It's the best way to do business."

"Can we wait until my lease is up?"

His eyebrows went up a bit, like he was impressed with my suggestion. "We absolutely can. We can wait as long as you want."

"It'll give me a little time to tell my family. Ease them into the idea of me living with a guy. And then I have to break it to Adler that I'm leaving. And that she can't come with me."

"Unfortunate, but true," Michael said with a smile. "I'm more of a one woman kind of guy."

"I'm seeing that. Are you having a good birthday?"

"I am. And I'm glad I'm spending it with you."

"Well there's one more part to all this. If you'll excuse me."

I ducked into the bedroom and changed into the white lace number I'd picked up a few days before. The top was more whimsical, a see–through, flowy fabric that covered me pretty well while still leaving almost nothing to the imagination. The bottoms matched, in theory, except they were crotchless, and kind of buttless, crafted for easy access. A final look in the mirror to fluff my hair before I joined Michael back in the kitchen. I grabbed the anal plug and the lube I'd ordered and a few condoms from his nightstand.

When I walked into the kitchen, Michael almost choked on his beer. He set his bottle back on the counter and managed to regain his composure. I waved the toy and the lubricant in the air as I came closer.

"I have to preface this by saying that I do not

think butt stuff should be reserved for birthdays only. You just have a really big dick and I wanted to work up to taking every inch of you."

"You know you might actually give me a heart attack."

I stepped between his legs. "How are you feeling now? Is your heart beating fast?"

"It is."

I put the plug and the lube in his hand. "Do you think you're feeling well enough to help me with this?"

"I think I'll survive. Turn around."

I did as he asked and tried to breathe when he pulled me tight against his chest. His hard dick pressed against my lower back as he kissed and bit his way down my neck to my shoulder.

"I had a whole seduction plan," I told him.

"I can see that. It's working. Let's move this to the couch."

We made our way into the living room portion of the massive space. Michael made himself comfortable on the lounger end of the couch and pulled me onto his lap. He kissed me gently at first and then his tongue invaded my mouth. I rubbed myself against him, positive I was leaving a wet spot along the bulge in his jeans. It was a desperate, shameless display, but I didn't care. I wanted him.

He pulled back just a bit, licking my lips. "I'm going to take it easy on you, but we're going to skip the plug tonight. Okay?"

I nodded frantically, reaching for his fly. "Yeah, okay." We went back to kissing, almost violently, like this was our last chance, like we would never get enough of each other.

I heard the lube cap pop somewhere in the distance and then I felt his fingers slicking the cool liquid over my tightest hole. He slipped one finger just inside and I was instantly reminded of how good it felt to be teased that way. I'd been down this road before, but it was a long time ago. And it wasn't with Michael.

He slipped another finger inside and this time, I pushed back, again and again until I was riding his hand. My clit was still throbbing. My whole body was more than worked up.

He handed me the bottle. "Get me ready," he said.

His dick was already rock hard between us so it was nothing to lean back and pour a healthy amount lube all over his head and shaft. I palmed him with both hands and spread the mess around. Michael didn't let me play with him for long though. He wanted in.

I draped myself against his chest, biting at the fabric on his shoulder as he started rubbing himself along my back entrance.

"Try and relax for me."

I took a deep breath and did as he asked, letting my whole body go as limp as possible. The first push felt so good. He was so perfectly thick, but I had to breathe through the pinches of pain as he went deeper. He went slow, bit by bit until he got past the tightest part and my body let him all the way in. I needed a moment to adjust. I felt so full, but my pussy kept clenching and clenching, wanting something of its own to grab on to.

He kissed my face. "Kay, talk to me. You alright?"

I nodded, feeling the ghost of an orgasm rushing through me. My tongue swept over my lips but I couldn't open my eyes. "I was just...thinking. If there were two of you."

His fingers brushed over my clit and then a little lower. He moved his hips at the same time, drawing himself out and pushing back in. Slowly. "You want me here too."

"Yeah," I said with a whimper.

"We'll have to do something about that," he said. And then he really started to move.

Along with my seduction scheme, I'd planned a few birthday weekend outings with Holger's help, but no. Michael and I spent the whole weekend in eating and fucking. He discovered I was ticklish and I discovered years of hard business had taught Michael to suppress all emotion, especially when I found the single square centimeter of ticklish skin on his body. It was on the left side of his neck.

Some time Sunday afternoon, I realized just how disgustingly cute we were and how well we worked together. He let me nap when I couldn't fuck or laugh anymore, and it didn't bother me at all when he was on the phone for forty-five minutes talking about an app redesign on Sunday morning while I was trying to watch cooking shows. I could do this with him, whatever it was, for a long time.

I spent the rest of the week doing my best to keep myself busy so I wouldn't think about his surprise party. I wasn't worried about the party itself. I was worried about the guest list. In his attempt to get me to understand just how important it was for me to get him to the venue, Ruben dropped the names for the more important people who were going to be there. Duke was performing, as was De'Bonay, my actual favorite singer. More celebs, general rich people, athletes, but I knew I'd only be star struck for a few minutes. Adler and Daniella were coming too, but obviously I wasn't worried about them. Michael's family was coming and Ruben thought it would be a perfect time for me to meet them.

Knowing Michael, if he didn't want me to meet his family, Ruben would never, ever put us in the same room, so I figured he was on board, which was a good sign, but that didn't change the fact that I was scared to death of what they would think. I wanted them to like me, not because I needed their approval. I was plenty secure in who I was, but I wanted them to like me for Michael. If they hated me I didn't want that tension to come between us. Michael didn't seem the type to dump me to make his family happy, especially since they lived in Michigan, but still. I wanted to avoid the drama.

Friday came so fast and before I knew it

Michael was picking me up for our "date". PJ had already been by to scoop up Daniella and Adler. They looked gorgeous in their gold dresses. I looked pretty great too. Sew-in redone and styled. Nails gelled to the nines and I managed to find a gold dress in almost the exact same style as the dress I was wearing the afternoon Michael and I met. The flowy maxi flattered all my curves. Michael smiled when he saw me.

The surprise portion of the evening went off without a hitch. The club was filled with guests, all wearing white and gold, and the minute we stepped in the door, Duke started performing a special rendition of "Happy Birthday". Michael was surprised and pleased. He looked at me, the pleasant shock written all over his face and I just smiled. Even wider when he kissed me before dragging me along to say his hellos. It took twenty minutes to make it over to the corner where Ruben and his family were waiting.

"Set up shop here," Ruben yelled to Michael over the music. "Let the rest of the guests come to you."

"Good call," he said back before he pulled me down onto the leather seats and introduced me to his sister Myra, his brother Matthew, and their spouses. They looked a little out of place only because all the other guest were so Hollywood and they looked like normal people dressed up for a night out. They all had the same black hair and the same blue eyes. Myra looked like a female version of Michael. Matthew had a different nose, but he and Michael had identical voices. It was almost eerie.

"Mom's not feeling great so Dad's home with her," Myra explained. So his parents were supposed to be there. "I told them we'd Facetime tomorrow morning."

"Yeah, yeah. That's fine. I'm just glad you guys are here." I saw a flicker of pain cross Michael's face. He was hoping his mother was doing better, or at least okay, but her not being able to make the trip told us that wasn't the case. Luckily Myra changed the subject.

"Okay, I'm going to do it. I'm going to embarrass him," she said to me.

I peered at Michael over my shoulder. "Please! Please do."

"Considering how little I actually talk to my brother, I have to say I have heard so much about you."

"Really?"

"Oh yeah." She leaned in and whisper-shouted in my ear. "He hasn't had it this bad since he was in high school."

"So, no pressure?" I laughed.

"Oh all the pressure you can handle, but I think you got this." And that's how Myra became my new best friend. No, but Myra was really cool. After things settled and Michael introduced me to five thousand more people, Daniella and Adler found us and we sat with Myra and Matthew's wife for most of the night. There were a few dance breaks, great finger foods, and plenty of girl talk, and then Michael's first business partner Steven gave a wonderful toast in his honor.

Michael begged off taking making his own speech, but no one was letting him get away. Ruben shoved the mic in his hand, a glass of champagne in the other, then pushed him up on one of the raised benches.

"I'll keep this short because I know most of you are here for the free boozes and the beautiful women. Not to hear me talk." That got a lot of laughs. "I just wanted to thank you all for coming out, thank you to my family for flying all this way to see me, and my lovely lady, Kayla for getting me here. It has been an amazing fifty years—fuck, I'm old—yeah. A lot of you have made this the most outstanding life a man could ask for. Here's to fifty years and fifty more."

When everyone raised their glasses I think I cheered the loudest.

Michael had to greet seven thousand more guests, but eventually De'Bonay took to the stage to perform and I dragged Michael to the dance floor. He wasn't the best dancer in the world, but he had a simple two-step down, and when I would periodically put it on him, he matched the rhythm of my hips instead of fumbling around or being distracted by the booty. Close to midnight the champagne was hitting us both. I needed water and he needed the restroom. I knew it was mistake separating, only because the number of people physically standing between us made the time before we were back in each other's hands exponentially longer. But nature called.

I made it over to the bar where I found

Daniella. She was Duke-less, but she was having a blast.

"This is seriously the best party I've ever been to. Tell Michael to turn fifty again next month."

"Maybe we can come up with a different reason to celebrate. Where's Adler?" I'd lost them both during the dance madness.

"Bathroom. She should be back soon. Unless there's a line."

"There's always a line."

But she came back a minute or so later. "No line?" I asked.

"Nope, used the men's. Let's go dance!" She grabbed both our hands, but I hung back.

"I'm just gonna stay put for Michael."

"Of course you are. Bye!" Adler said. Daniella waved as she let Adler tow her away.

I downed two glasses of water and ordered a third and another glass for Michael before he came back. He looked upset.

I handed him his water. He thanked me and took a deep swig, but still, upset. He wouldn't look at me and he always looked at me. Instead he was scanning the room, clearly looking for someone.

"Honey, you okay?" I asked.

"Yeah. We'll talk about it tomorrow."

"Anything I can do to help?" The tone of my voice must have snapped him out of it because he finally looked at me. He put down his glass and pulled me closer with an arm around my waist.

"You're here with me tonight. That's all I want."

"That's all I want too."

"Have I told you how beautiful you look tonight?" he asked.

"Yes, but you can say it again."

Michael leaned down and brushed his lips across my neck. "You looking fucking beautiful, Kayla."

Another song started up. "Let's sit the next few out."

"Okay." Michael wrangled us two more champagnes and we made off for a private corner. We were able to people watch and make out for seven whole minutes before more friends of the birthday boy found us and wanted to catch up. And so it went for the rest of the night, but I was with Michael so, even with the interruptions, I thought it was pretty perfect.

Chapter Eight

I was hungover as shit the next morning. I had more champagne than I'd ever consumed before and then we ended up at some burger spot after hours. I was dehydrated and gross, but all I needed was some water and pancakes and sunglasses because, if I remembered correctly, we were supposed to meet Michael's family for brunch. We'd stayed in the hotel above the club. One of the super fancy places on Sunset that I'd only driven by before and never imagined I'd spend the night in. Of course Ruben and Holger had hooked it up and made sure our hotel room was stocked with clean clothes and condoms. I'd started on the pill, but we were still covering our bases.

Oh the sex had been a complete mess, but one of those good messes that reassured me Michael and I could both perform under the influence. The next morning when I finally peeled my eyes open and rolled over, looking for some water, I found Michael sitting up on the edge of the bed. He was still naked, his long hair trailing down his back.

"Morning," I said. My voice sounded like shit. Still, Michael looked over his shoulder and smiled.

"Morning." The smiled faded. "I have to talk to you about something that happened last night."

"Oh god. What did I do?"

"Nothing." he stood up and stepped into his

boxers. It would take me a minute to rally, but it looked like this conversation was going to take a brunch-time quickie right off the table. "You didn't do anything. I have to talk to you about your roommate."

I flopped back on the bed. "Oh fuck. What the shit did Adler do?"

"She grabbed my dick."

At that I sat right the fuck up. "What?"

"But that was after she offered to step in when I was done with you and before she offered to have a threesome with us when I told her I had no plans to be done with you."

I almost threw up. "I—"

"Can we agree that this is not something I would make up?"

"I—," I swallowed the hurl in my throat and tried again. "Yeah. I know you wouldn't do that. I'm just—I don't think Adler would say something like that. Actually no. I do, but just not to you. She knows how I feel about you."

"I don't think she does. And clearly she has no idea how I feel about you." I looked up as the words left his mouth. Michael was pissed. Like really pissed. I'd never seen him angry like this before. "I'm not gonna bullshit you, Kayla. I love you and I have to say this because I love you and I want you in my life. I take the relationships in my life very seriously."

"I know you do."

He shook his head then looked at the ceiling. I'd never seen him frazzled like this before either. He was always so sure, so confident, but I could tell he was working up the nerve to tell me something awful.

"Adler's not allowed in my life anymore. She's definitely not allowed in my house anymore. I don't want her around."

"So you're saying I can't be friends with her anymore? You want me to pick between you and Adler? My best friend?"

"I'm not asking you to pick. You can stay friends with her if that's what you want. I barely know the girl so I won't act like I know what her friendship means to you, but I don't want her around me. She grabbed my fucking dick." I closed my eyes and let the dread wash over me. Michael was completely right. I put myself in his shoes and if one of his friends had groped me, and suggested that... I didn't want to think about the particulars. I wouldn't feel comfortable around that person either and I would be seriously questioning what Michael saw in them.

He leaned against the hotel desk. He was giving me space to make a decision and, knowing Michael, he would want my answer soon.

I hated crying, but the tears started running. Michael finally came over to the bed and pulled me into his arms. "I'm sorry."

"No, no. It's not you. Actually it is you, a little. You're so blunt and honest. I'm not used to that. Usually people sugar-coat shit, or exaggerate a little. Or lie."

"I know. I—I shouldn't talk to you like that though. It works in the boardroom, but this isn't business. This is about us."

"No. I want you to be honest with me. I just—

Adler's my best friend."

"I know, baby." He kissed my face and pulled me closer. "It's your call. I can't—"

"I know."

We stayed in bed a little longer, but eventually climbed into the shower, together. I asked Michael if he still wanted me to come to brunch. He said he and Myra wouldn't have it any other way.

Brunch was fine. It was more than fine. Myra was hilarious when she was hungover and it was nice to see Michael relax and talk with his brother. I could see what he meant about needing and wanting normal. His family was so normal and mid-West and everyone Michael usually hung out with was so not. It made me happy to see him so at ease and in his true element, but the whole time I couldn't help but think, *what the hell am I going to do about Adler?* Michael knew it was on my mind. He didn't say anything but, every once in a while, he would give me that look, that look that told me we'd be okay, no matter what.

I believed Michael. I knew everyone had a twinge of Satan inside, but Michael was not that kind of evil or fucked up to make something up just to get me to end a friendship with someone he barely saw and who didn't actually monopolize my time. And as far as he knew the craziest thing Adler had done was lure me to the Arrangements website and we knew how that was playing out. I just didn't understand why this was happening.

As we were waiting for the check, Adler sent me a text, a picture of Duke and Daniella leaving the club. Michael and I were in the background.

It's from Page Six!
Headline's about Duke and his "date", but you're kinda famous!

It was a little weird and exciting to see myself in a pap photo. Ruben told me it might happen, but after more than a month of being completely ignored by any member of the social press that might take an interest in Michael and his love life, I'd forgotten all about Ruben's warning. I was so drunk in the picture I didn't remember it being taken. Still. I looked great. I was able to enjoy that simple pleasure for ten seconds before I remembered that Adler had sent the picture and was probably waiting for a response. I put my phone on silent and slipped it into my purse.

"Do you want me to stay?" Michael slid a gentle hand around the back of my neck. His family had plans to sightsee and hit a show at the Pantages. Michael said we could spend the rest of the weekend together, maybe go out on his boat or hang by the pool, but I knew the longer I waited to talk to Adler the worse it would get.

I looked over at him then kissed his wrist. "No. This could be a quick conversation or it could be long drawn out thing, but I know I'll feel a certain kind of way if I know you're out here waiting."

"Okay. Well you know how to get me."

"You're just a text away."

"Exactly."

I kissed him then slipped out of the car and headed inside. The elevator ride was too short. I kept playing out the whole fight in my head over and over again. I'd confront and she'd deny or downplay. Deny and downplay. Or condescend and try to convince me I was blowing things out of proportion. She bumped into Michael by the bathroom. Nothing more. Adler and I hadn't gotten into many fights over the course of our time as friends and all of those arguments had been about stupid stuff like dishes in the sink or the TV being too loud. Nothing serious. Nothing to do with a serious boyfriend.

When I got to the apartment Adler wasn't there. No note of course, because I wasn't her mom and she probably thought I'd be off with Michael until further notice. She didn't come home for hours and by the time she walked in I felt the exact way I didn't want to feel. My anxiety and fear had had too long to fester.

"Whoa. You okay?" she asked, as she dropped her purse by the door.

I let out a deep breath and sat up a little straighter. "What did you say to Michael last night?"

"Huh? Happy Birthday? I don't even know. I barely talked to him. Why?"

"You didn't say or do anything to him outside of the bathroom?"

"Oh! That." Then she had the nerve to look offended. "It wasn't that big of a deal, Kay. I just asked him—"

"To call you when he kicked me to the curb?"

"No, come on. I didn't say it like that."

"What did you say? And why did you say it?"

"I just said that he had options. I said I was cool if he was down for a threesome."

"You grabbed him by the crotch. Christ, Adler. Why? You know how I feel about him."

"I know how you think you feel about him, but come on. He took you on as a sugar baby. He's fucking fifty. You just like him because he's sweet to you. You like everyone who's sweet to you."

"You say it like it's a bad thing."

"It is if it blinds you to reality. Michael is a billionaire. Michael has made it our whole lives, times two, without settling down. Michael met you at a sugar party. Where do you think this is going to go?"

"Wherever we want this to go. We're…"

"Holy shit. You think he's in love with you."

"What?"

"Kayla. You don't keep guys like this. You enjoy them and then you set them free." She opened her arms in a sweeping motion that would have been real funny under any other circumstances.

"Whatever. He didn't appreciate what you did or what you said, you're not welcome around him anymore."

"Is this you talking or him?"

"It's both of us. He doesn't want you around and I—"

"You what?"

"I don't want to be friends with someone who comes on to my boyfriend." I didn't think I would actually feel that way, but I did. I'd never been hurt like this before.

"I hope you hear yourself. You're going to let your weepy feelings for your literal Sugar Daddy that you've been talking to for like twenty minutes tell you that we shouldn't be friends anymore."

"No, Adler. What the hell? Michael is my literal boyfriend and you literally came on to him. Why would you do that?"

"Because he's a fucking Sugar Daddy, Kay. Are. You. Kidding. Me?" I realized that Adler's opinion of me might be wading in some murky water, but the real problem was how she saw Michael. She didn't respect him at all. He was just a hot walking bag of money with a dick attached. She didn't respect Michael or anything about him, and she was actually shocked that I did. I stood up. I couldn't be around her anymore.

"I gotta go."

"To Michael's? I'm sure he wants to her about our post-adolescent lady squabble." I just looked at her. She'd managed to insult all three of us at once.

I went into my room and locked the door. Part of me wanted to text Michael and ask him to come back and get me, but I was too raw to deal with him and his unfiltered honesty. I called Daniella.

She listened patiently as I blubbered on, telling her what happened. The way she sighed didn't comfort me. "I knew she was going to try that."

"You did?"

"She hit on Duke too, but we're not as serious as you and Michael. We're just kinda sorta talking and running into each other. You and Michael are legit."

"You think so?"

"Oh my god, yes. Kayla. You should see the way he looks at you." Daniella laughed a little. "It's gross. He like loooooooves you."

"He dropped the L bomb this morning."

"God, I bet it was all perfect too. Was his hair all messy?"

I laughed this time. "Yeah, but we were mid-fight, kinda. I just don't—what the fuck do I do about Adler? Michael is done with her. Like done-done and I don't trust her."

"Can I be honest?"

"Wouldn't have it any other way," I said, waiting for another layer to this shit sandwich of misery.

"How do I put this? Adler's your friend. Not mine."

"Jesus."

"I mean she always says fucked up things. And this isn't the first time you've asked what to do about her. Yeah, before it was silly stuff, like how she ate all your food or made a joke that was borderline offensive, but I never ask people what I should do about you. And that's how friendships should be. Friends are there to support you. You know, share in the good times. Not make you question why you have them around."

"I know."

"I don't want to tell you what to do, but I can tell Michael cares about you a lot and if Adler is trying to get between you guys just to prove that she can, well…" I could just see her shrugging on the other end of the phone. She was right. There wasn't much more to say about it.

Daniella and I talked a little while longer. She told me how things were weird with Duke, but she wanted to keep seeing him if he was up for it.

"Well I'm here if you need someone to give him a stern talking-to."

"You're always first in my contacts. You okay?"

"Yeah, I'm fine. I just have to break up with Adler."

"Yes, you do. Don't wait. Just rip the Band-Aid off." Daniella was right, but that was easier said than done.

Relying on a driver makes it real easy to forget addresses. It also prevents you from learning addresses in the first place. I walked right out of the apartment without saying a word to Adler, who was on the phone with Sienna talking shit about me as I passed through the living room. That pissed me off enough to fuel my rage halfway to Santa Monica and Adler's shitty text almost got me to the PCH.

Just gonna leave like that? her text said. I was too angry to wait to respond. I pulled over and shot her a text back.

The lease is up in six months. Do what you want with that information. I hit send then I silenced her notifications.

And then I called Holger. I needed the address to the house.

The sun was going down as I pulled up the last incline to Michael's house. I imagined Holger waiting by the security cameras because the gates swung open the moment I reached them. And Michael was there, walking out the front door just as I put my car in park. Hair pulled up, barefoot, in a tattered UCLA hoodie and boxers and still as gorgeous as ever. I walked right up to him. He took my cheeks in his hands. I knew my eyes were still red and puffy. That must have been why he kissed my lids before he made his familiar trip to my dimples and my lips.

"Didn't go well?" he asked.

I shook my head. "She thought I was using you 'cause that's what she'd planned to do."

"What do you want to do now?"

"Be with you. That's what I want."

"Here."

"Yeah." We had to work out some details, but it seemed silly to go on another apartment hunt. I loved Michael and he wanted me to live with him. The move was already on the books. Why not move it up a few months?

"I'll send Holger over to get your stuff in the morning."

"Okay. But there's one more thing I have to do."

"We have to call you mother."

"Yup. We have to call my mom."

"Tomorrow?"

"Please. I just want to lie down. And make out with you."

Michael's chest shook as he let out a little chuckle. "I think we can arrange that."

I had to remember not to roll my eyes. My parents could see us, but my mom was giving new meaning to the third degree. We had a plan. I knew I'd go nuts hanging out around the house with Holger while Michael was at the office every day, so I would keep looking for jobs and then enroll in classes in the fall. I also wanted to make some money of my own. Michael was more than generous and I knew I couldn't contribute to his mortgage or the upkeep on the jet, but I wanted to contribute to my own expenses. It was the best way for me.

It wasn't exactly working for my parents though. I was an adult and they weren't so strict and controlling to try to fly out to California just to yank me out of Michael's house, but they had their beliefs and their opinions about how a man and a woman ought to conduct their private lives.

"Michael, you see why I'm worried," my mom said. We had her and my dad on video chat. Kiara showed them how to use her tablet to call us and then they'd promptly kicked her out of the room. My dad was taking the news of Michael and I living together in stride, but my mom had almost shit a duck. "I met her last boyfriend's parents before we let him come stay the summer. And now you're telling me you're living together and this is the first time I've seen your face."

"He wasn't my last boyfriend, mom."

"He was the last boyfriend I knew about. I just want Michael to know—"

"Mom, he knows."

Finally my dad chimed in. "Michael, I do not believe a couple should live together before they're married, but I know things are different these days. I'm going to take your word that *you're* going to take care of my Kayla."

"I will, Mr. Davis."

My mom wasn't done yet though. "And you can also see where I'd have a problem with an older white man trying to shack up with my young, black daughter."

"Oh my goodness. Mom! This isn't a church play. Michael is not a confederate sympathizer. We're dating. We're living together and everything is cool and not racist and creepy."

Michael was horrified, but he and my father were both trying not to laugh.

"We'll let you two go," my dad said. He knew my mom had hit her rational limit. "We'd like to meet you some time soon, Michael."

"If you'll have me, I'd love to come down with Kayla to visit."

"You're sleeping in separate bedrooms when you get here. Shacking up with an old white man. I see the gray in that beard. Your daddy doesn't even have that much grey hair—" My mom was still muttering to herself when she dipped out of the frame and left the room.

"Our door is open," my dad said. "Kayla Renee, you call us next week."

"I will Dad. Love you."

"Love you too." I waited a few seconds while my dad figured out how to end the video chat. Then I turned to Michael.

"It gets worse than that. I have two sisters, remember. And they are just like my mom."

"I can handle it."

"You sure? You can't buy your way out of that madness, buddy."

"Then I'll just have to win them over by taking really good care of you."

"I think I can handle that. Dinner then butt stuff by the fire pit?"

Michael snorted then kissed me on my lips. "Anything for my lady. Lead the way."

The End

What's Next from Rebekah

Want more from Kayla and Michael? Check out the beginning of their next chapter in SO RIGHT.

Chapter One

I woke up feeling so good. I stretched, pulling the covers back up to my bare shoulders, basking in the warmth of our sheets. If you asked me a year ago if I was happy, I would have said yes. A year ago, I had a job that took care of all my needs, and a cute apartment. I had a roommate who I thought was a great friend, loving parents and twin siblings who thought I was the coolest big sister in the world. The parents still loved me and my sisters still thought I was pretty neat, but I'd lost my job, and then me and my roommate almost ran out of money and decided that the fine life of sugaring was right for us. It absolutely wasn't, but then I met him, Michael Bradbury, for real for real Internet billionaire and now everything was different.

A year ago I didn't know butt from crap about happiness. Now, I had a job I actually wanted. The roommate who turned out to be less than a friend was out of my life. With a little help from said billionaire I was able to rescue my best friend Daniella from her boring corporate job at Telett Wireless and together we had opened Cards by K&D, a greeting card company for the millennial set. Our first official line, Queer Qards by K&D, was due to launch in a few months at L.A. Pride. I had no idea just how awesome it could be to work for yourself and *that* made me pretty damn happy. And then there was Michael.

On the surface, Michael and I made no damn sense. There was the age gap and the bank account gap, and the fact that some dudes don't like girls as thick and juicy as me, and some black girls like me didn't mess with older white guys, but beneath it all we were both just two big nerds who got excited about bad food and things like graphic design and user experience. Before him I had no idea what it felt like to be so in love. I had no idea what it was like to be in a relationship with someone so considerate and so kind. Now when people waxed poetic about soul mates and true partners I knew they weren't lying because I had found that in Michael. He also asked me to move in with him so now I had an even nicer, cuter place to live.

I rolled over to the sound of his fingers moving across his keyboard. Didn't matter if we had a late night or not, didn't matter that it was Saturday either. For Michael, every morning it was early to rise and right to work. The sun was up and I'm sure birds were chirping somewhere; I just couldn't hear them through the double paned windows of his Malibu home. Our home. But the smell of breakfast wafting down the hall made the perfect scene complete.

We had plans for our Saturday morning, adorable couple-y things to do, but it was still too early for Michael to look so good. His long black hair was sporting a few more grays, catching up with his salt and pepper beard and mustache. His thick locks were down, falling around his shoulders, hanging down his back, still all messed up from the great sex we'd had the night before. I knew I was still feeling the effects of our love making turned rowdy fucking. My thighs were a bit sore, and my pussy was still wet. It was a bird chirping kind of day.

"Good morning," I said, my voice a little scratchy from sleep. I couldn't help but smile when he glanced over at me. Those blue eyes.

"Morning, baby. Are you excited?" His lips tipped up a bit at the corner, his version of a smile. He was always so calm and introspective. Only a few people in his life got to see the real thing. Only I got to see him this naked.

"Do you want my honest answer?"

"No. Lie to me. All day long. I hate honesty in a woman."

"I know. Liars are where it's at. Um, yeah. I'm stupid excited."

"Well then. I think we should get going." He leaned over and lightly kissed my cheek before he closed his laptop and slid it down to the foot of our massive bed. I'd just recently started calling it our bed. And our house. I'd been living with Michael in his sprawling modern home in Malibu for almost ten months, but it took me a long time to get over the fact that I wasn't just a visitor. I lived with my boyfriend and it was totally fine for me to make myself comfortable.

And I would have been completely comfortable if Michael's house—our house—wasn't ninety-seven percent glass. The massive windows that made up most of the exterior walls afforded an amazing view of the ocean and the mountains of Malibu, but at night it also felt like a horrifying glass box that was just begging to be burgled. Michael travelled a lot, leaving me alone with his housekeeper, Holger.

I loved Holger's big German ass, but when he was done with his work for the day, his time was his and he spent that time in the pool house. I couldn't ask him to spend the night up in the main house every night Michael was away. He didn't get paid to babysit me. We had a big fence and a gate that could only be opened with a seven-digit code, and Holger could probably hear me screaming if an intruder got by all of that, but there was only one thing that would make me feel completely safe, and Michael agreed.

I reached under the sheets and drew my freshly manicured nails up his toned thigh. "Is Holger still mad?"

"Do you want to go feel him up like this? Butter him up a little?"

"I would if I thought it would work."

"It's that serious, huh?"

"Yes. Baby. We need a puppy."

"You're right," he said with a firm nod. He pursed his lips. "We should get some food in that belly and then hit the road."

I watched Michael as he climbed out of bed, leaving my hand sad and lonely on the warm spot he left in the sheets. I took every inch of him in. The curtains were drawn, but our bedroom was nicely lit by the morning sun. That body. It was sinful for a man at any age. Perfect ass, stacked and toned.

Muscles and tattoos, tanned skin dusted with dark hairs in all the right places. He came around my side of the bed, heavy dick hanging between his legs, probably a little hard from the way I had just been touching his leg. He headed toward the bathroom, and a shower, I guessed, but like he said we still had plenty of time before the shelters opened.

I reached out and caught his fingertips before he could get away. He stopped walking and looked down at me. "Am I being too demanding if I ask you to come back to bed?"

"It depends on what you want me to do if I get back in bed." He moved a little closer and toyed with my fingers.

"Share your penis with me," I said with a pout, watching as his eyes narrowed with just the slightest bit of annoyance.

"Last night, after you came the third time—"

"The fourth. What? I came like five times really, but like four big ones. But do go on. You were saying," I said smiling back with my toothiest grin.

"After you came, I was nowhere near done, but last night when we were coming back from dinner, what did you tell me?"

"I may have said that I wanted to get up early so we could be the first ones to the shelter."

"That's exactly what you said. You can't keep toying with my penis like this," he said, putting his hands on his perfectly sculpted hips. I looked him up and down, starting at those hips and then down lower to the erection that looked like it wanted to come out to play. My eyes wandered up some more to the massive eagle tattoo whose wings covered half his chest and half of his back. And I looked further up, to his perfectly full lips.

"I'm sorry I'm so mean. Here, let me repay you before we go." I gave his hand a solid tug and pulled him back under the covers with me. When he was comfortable I did the only sensible thing and climbed on top of him. It took nothing to slide a little lower so my pussy was rubbing along the length of his quickly hardening dick. My eyes closed as his hands traced the length of my spine. I shifted against him some more, growing wetter every second.

"I'll stop being a dick," I said quietly before I leaned down and kissed his perfect lips. There was a faint hint of sweetened coffee on his breath. I didn't give him shit for being up *and* caffeinated.

"Good," he said when I pulled back just enough. "You know I'll give you whatever you want." I was being a dick still, teasing him, rubbing myself up and down all over him.

"And I'll give you whatever you want."

"Then stop fucking teasing me." That was enough to make me come, how he could go from sweet to filthy in no seconds flat.

"I think I need some assistance."

"You always seem to catch me in my most charitable moods. Let me see what I can do for you."

His hands moved down to my waist, lifting me just enough so my wet slit opened for him. He was big and thick, but every time my pussy took every inch of him.

I sat up just enough to place my hard nipples

right on his mouth, my breath rushing through my teeth as he teased me with his tongue. I couldn't help but ride him hard, couldn't resist fucking myself fast and rough on his thick length.

This was what Saturday mornings were for. Caffeinated kisses and perfect sex.

"Did I mention how excited I am? We're getting a dog, dude," I said as the first hints of an orgasm slid over me. Michael's laughter sputtered around my boob.

"Kayla. Please. Focus." His teeth scraped my tender skin and then he bit down. There was no way Holger didn't hear me coming from the kitchen.

I did want us to be the first people at the West Los Angeles Animal Shelter, but by the time we stopped fucking and by the time I finished repairing the damaged I'd done to my hair by not sleeping in a scarf, I knew we'd probably be the second or third people there. Luckily we'd already picked up a crate and other odds and ends to help our new puppy settle in. Holger was vehemently against bringing animals into the house, but he lost the argument two to one. We were going to get that fucking dog.

I came out into the kitchen and found Michael and Holger glued to the TV. "What's going on?" I asked.

"Good morning, sweet heart." Holger always

separated the words. "Here's your breakfast." He set a plate with a massive omelet and some fruit at the table setting right next to the remains of Michael's breakfast.

Michael glanced away from the TV for a moment, flashing me a warm smile as he held out his hand. I grabbed my plate and came around the other side of his stool so I could stand between his legs while he watched TV. Some player from the Miami Flames was talking about showing up that night for the fans.

"What's the haps?" I asked.

"Steven just texted me and told me to turn it on."

When we met, Michael had been in talks to purchase L.A.'s NBA team from its aging owner, but at the last minute the deal fell through when the owner's son decided he wanted to keep the team in the family. Michael had been disappointed, but he'd shaken it off and moved on to other things, like investing in my business with Daniella. Still, he'd been a lifelong basketball fan, and whenever he was in town we used his courtside season tickets. He always followed the action in the league.

The program cut back to the woman at the broadcast desk. "That was Ladarian Thomas sharing his thoughts on tonight's game against Dallas. Again for those just tuning in, this morning it has been confirmed that Miami Flames owner, Jonathan Taylor Wayne, has been arrested in connection with the contract killing of Orlando resident Arnold Foster over alleged gambling debts. We are expecting a statement from the league commissioner shortly."

"Holy shit," I said under my breath.

"Yeah. That's pretty serious," Michael said as he gave me a little affectionate squeeze on my side.

We continued watching the coverage of the story, as another reporter picked up the report. In addition to being the team's owner, Jonathan Taylor Wayne, who also owned majority stock in Clast Airlines, had apparently been involved in a small but high-stakes gambling ring. I hadn't heard about Arnold Foster's murder, probably because it hadn't made the national news, and after pulling his name up on my phone I found some more details. He'd been shot to death in his car while driving through Orlando three months ago, execution style. Apparently the triggerman had come forward and named the owner of Miami's team as the one who had hired him. It was some movie of the week type shit. When it got to the point where they were rehashing information we already knew, we finished up breakfast and our coffee.

"We'll be back in a couple hours," Michael told Holger as he slipped on his hoodie. Casually dressed Michael was just as hot as all-business Michael.

"Wonderful."

"Cheer up, man. A dog will bring much needed energy to this place."

"I am completely satisfied with the level of energy Kayla has brought to your home." I tried not to laugh in Holger's face. Six foot six and nearly as wide, mohawk and all, and there he was huffing and puffing like an exhausted child.

"Sorry. She wants a dog. She's getting a dog."

Holger glared at me for a moment before a small smile cracked under his handlebar mustache. "Well yes. Resisting the desires of that dimpled face is a fruitless effort."

"We can name it after you if you want," I teased.

"Absolutely not. Just help me clean up after it. I signed on for one man. Now I have a man, a woman, and a mongrel to look after."

"And you are nicely compensated for all of your hard work," Michael reminded him.

"Now is not the time to bring up those types of particulars," Holger huffed as he moved our breakfast dishes over to the sink.

Michael rolled his eyes then took my hand. "We'll be back."

There were a few other people when we arrived at the animal shelter, but I think we had first dibs on the dogs. The family in front of us in line had a very hyper kid, around five or six years old, who was over the moon about picking out a new cat. When it was our turn Michael might have ribbed me a little as I tried to play it cool when the woman behind the counter asked how she could help us.

"Can you show us what you have in a puppy? A large breed perhaps?" Michael said like he was ordering a fine bottle of wine. I rolled my eyes, but laughed with the shelter attendant.

"We do, actually." She pointed us toward the sound of dozens of barking dogs and told us to have a look.

There were so many dogs. I felt terrible, but short of opening our own dog rescue there wasn't much I could do. Michael stopped at the third stall where the cutest grey pit bull puppy was yapping at the fence.

"Penny. Done. Found my dog," Michael said.

"Oh my god, she's so cute."

"She's mine. Keep it moving, sister."

"What? She's great. Let's take her. A pit will murder anything that comes through the door." This was the dog I needed.

"You seemed to want something in the way of a small horse. Keep looking." I looked at him for a second, but he ignored me, squatting down so little Penny could lick his fingers through the fence. "Hey girl," he cooed sweetly.

"Oh. My. God. You want your own puppy. I thought you just wanted one."

"A man is allowed to change his mind."

"A man is full of shit is what he is," I laughed.

Just then one of Michael's phones rang. He straightened instantly and pulled his business cell out of his pocket.

"This is Michael—She's mine. Back off." I glared at him and kept moving down the line. "Richard, hi. Sorry. My girlfriend and I are picking up a dog." I looked back trying to figure out which

Richard he was talking to. He did business with like five. Michael nodded toward the exit then headed outside to take his call.

Like the woman said, there was a mutt puppy that must have been part Newfoundland. It looked more bear cub than dog. It was so cute, but I could just imagine all that fur everywhere. Holger would kill us. There was also some Cujo looking creature that lunged at the fence, barking it's fucking face off as soon as I walked by. I screamed and jumped out of the way like I was at a damn haunted house.

As soon as my brain reminded me of the fence between me and the monster, I moved on to the last stall. My heart still beating in my throat and shoes nearly filled with fear pee, I found another shorthaired puppy, silver with black and white spots and solid black ears and feet. He was a baby, but he had the big clumsy puppy paws that just told you one day you'd be able to throw a saddle on him and rent him out to kiddie parties. The name Patch was on his cage.

He came over to the gate and jumped, trying to lick my hand. He'd make a lousy guard dog, but at least I wouldn't be alone. Michael still wasn't back so I walked back up front.

"I think we're going to take Penny and Patch," I told the woman behind the desk.

"Great!"

Michael came back as they were getting the paperwork ready. I didn't like the frown on his face. "What's going on?"

"Nothing. That was Richard Sands. I might

have to go to New York. We'll talk about it in the car."

"'Kay," I said, letting it go. We didn't need to talk shop at the animal shelter counter, but I grabbed his hand anyway.

Penny was good to go, shots and all, but we had to make an appointment to get Patch fixed in the next few months. And then we had two extremely rambunctious puppies on our hands.

"Holger is gonna kill us," I said after we walked them around the block and got them settled on the blanket we'd put down in the backseat of Michael's G-Class. I climbed back up front and fastened my seatbelt. "So what's going on?"

The frown came back to his face. "They want me to purchase Miami."

"Really? That's great, right? This is what you wanted."

"I wanted to purchase an L.A. team. Miami is a different situation. And the L.A. deal was simple. This is a fucking PR disaster." Michael handled press just fine under pressure, but the kind of press he did was interviews with tech magazines and the occasional rich people publications. He'd never been involved in a legit scandal. Still, I wanted to encourage him to go for it.

One, Michael was actually a good man and with his calm, caring personality and his freakish ability to focus on the right thing, I thought he would be the perfect person to bring the team back together after John Taylor Wayne had his day in court. But this was his call and all I could do was support his choice.

That's how we did things on Team Bradbury-Davis. Mutual support. It felt so good.

He was quiet for a while as we made our way back to the PCH, but suddenly he pulled out his phone. Ruben's name flashed across the dashboard.

"Yes, sir." The voice of Michael's assistant and my good friend chimed through the speakers.

"Hey, sorry to bother you. I have to fly to New York tonight. I need you to come. Am I fucking up your plans?"

"Tonight?" I said a little too loud, my stomach dropping. I instantly wanted to take back my whining, but the puppies!

"Is that my Kay-Kay?"

"Hey Ruben."

"Did you get the puppy?"

"Puppies. Michael cracked and got one for himself."

"Oh yay! Take pictures. I'll come over and play with them when we get back."

"You'll see Penny tonight," Michael added. "Let the crew know we'll be plus one dog."

"What?" Ruben and I said at the same time.

"She's not a Pomeranian, babe. She's a pit bull," I reminded him. Penny was plenty small to carry, but...

"You got a pit bull puppy?" Ruben asked, his shock justified. Pits had a bad rep for sure, but even I didn't have to struggle to imagine just how much more intimidating people would find Michael with a pit bull in his board meetings.

"The sign said she was pit bull/lab mix, but

yeah, and another mutt. PJ and I'll pick you up at seven."

"Great. See you then."

The call ended and Michael wasted no time reaching over and rubbing the back of my neck. "I'm sorry. I have to do this. Richard wants me to meet with the commissioner, just to talk. I think this gambling ring, the conspiracy, everything might be bigger than Wayne."

"Like within the NBA?"

"Yes. They want to get the process of replacing him started immediately."

"Yeah, okay. You should definitely go." I looked back at the puppies, kissing Michael's wrist as I turned my head. Patch was relaxed, looking up at me with his big green eyes, ignoring Penny while she sniffed and batted at his ear. "I'll see if Daniella wants to come over."

"Sounds like a good idea. Are her and Duke still—"

"I don't know." My best friend and Michael's good friend were sort of an item. Problem was, Duke Stone, international pop star and mega producer had a crazier schedule than Michael's. Combine that with Daniella's fear of getting her heart broken and you had the perfect recipe for a will they, won't they. I pulled out my phone and sent her a text.

Busy tonight?

Nope. Watching movies with sister. Duke's on timeout.

You and sister want to come over tonight? You can tell

me what he did and meet my new puppy.

Hell yes. I could use some puppy time.

Michael would be leaving around six so I told them to come around five thirty so they could catch Penny before Michael took her on her first airplane ride. With my evening resolved, I sent Holger a text.

Coming home with two puppies. I'm sorry.

He sent a series of emoticons that made how he felt about our impulse grab perfectly clear.

About the Author

Rebekah was raised in Southern New Hampshire and now lives in Southern California with a great human, one cat whom she loves dearly and another cat she wants to take back to the shelter.

Her interests include Wonder Woman collectibles, cookies, James Taylor, whatever Nicki Minaj is doing at any given moment, quality hip-hop, football, American muscle cars, large breed dogs, and the ocean. When she's not working, writing, reading, or sleeping, she is watching HGTV and cartoons, or taking dance classes. If given the chance, she will cheat at UNO.

You can find more stories by Rebekah at rebekahweatherspoon.com

CPSIA information can be obtained
at www.ICGtesting.com
Printed in the USA
FSOW02n0916190717
36614FS